'Did I say how pretty you look this morning?'

Joe whispered. 'I expect this is going to be the best holiday I've ever had.'

He kissed her on the cheek. Alicia's heart skipped a beat, and her breath caught in her chest. A pleasant warmth surged through her veins.

A half second later, Alicia realised her grandfather was watching them and grinning from ear to ear. Of course. Joe was doing this for Grandpa Roger's benefit. She'd almost forgotten it was an act. For a moment, she'd become a part of the fantasy.

Joe smiled that sexy smile of his before giving her another kiss. Then he strode out of the room, whistling softly under his breath.

Alicia stood beside the open door a moment or two longer, thankful for the cool air on her skin. Her head told her his words were nothing more than lines, but her heart longed to believe they were true...

Dear Reader,

Welcome to Special Edition™!

We're very excited that two brand-new **Montana** stories in one volume, *A Montana Christmas*, leads off the holiday line-up, and the next **Montana** story follows next month and comes from eternal favourite Laurie Paige.

Our **That's My Baby!** title this month is *Stand-In Mum* from the talented pen of Marie Ferrarella and should make all baby lovers satisfied. There will be a follow-up title in due course, too.

Two seasonal books where two unwitting men find out they are fathers—well after the event!—are heading your way from Allison Leigh and Trisha Alexander. Both are part of family series and well worth seeking out.

There's another book that springs from a family we've met before, *Wyoming Wildcat*, where Grace McBride Kramer finds a man who's a 'keeper'. And the last book in this Christmas line-up is *Daddy Claus* on the popular theme of a pretend marriage that soon becomes more.

We hope you'll love them all,

The Editors

Daddy Claus

ROBIN LEE HATCHER

SILHOUETTE

SPECIAL EDITION®

*All the characters in this book have no existence outside the imagination
of the author, and have no relation whatsoever to anyone bearing the
same name or names. They are not even distantly inspired by any
individual known or unknown to the author, and all the incidents are
pure invention.*

*First published in Great Britain 2000
Silhouette Books, Eton House, 18-24 Paradise Road,
Richmond, Surrey TW9 1SR*

© Robin Lee Hatcher 1999

ISBN 0 373 24288 3

23-1200

*Printed and bound in Spain
by Litografia Rosés S.A., Barcelona*

ROBIN LEE HATCHER

discovered her vocation as a writer after many years of reading everything she could put her hands on, including the backs of cereal boxes and ketchup bottles. However, she's certain there are better plots and fewer calories in her books than in puffed rice and hamburgers. A past president of Romance Writers of America, Robin is the author of over twenty-five novels. Her books have won numerous awards, including the prestigious Romance Writers of America RITA Award.

In those rare moments when she isn't working on a new book, Robin and her husband, Jerry, like to escape to their cabin in the mountains of Idaho with their border collie and Shetland sheepdog. Hobbies are nearly non-existant since she sold her first book, but she enjoys the occasional golf game (don't ask about the scores!), loves movies (both old and new) and live musical theatre and is a season-ticket holder with the Idaho Shakespeare Festival. She also loves to spend time with her two daughters and three young grandchildren.

Prologue

Private Internet Chat Room
November 6, Midnight

MtnMama: I don't know what I'll do.

SkiBum: May I make a suggestion? You could tell your grandfather the truth.

MtnMama: I can't do that. It would break his heart. I only lied in the first place to protect him. He was so sick. No one thought he would survive his heart attack. And even when he did, I never *dreamed* the doctor would allow him to travel. I thought I would have more time.

SkiBum: "Oh, what a tangled web we weave, when first we practice to deceive!"

MtnMama: Very funny.

SkiBum: Sorry.

SkiBum: :-\

SkiBum: Thought Sir Walter Scott had a good point.

MtnMama: Not in this circumstance. Grandpa's from the old school. You know. Marriage is for a lifetime. There's never been a divorce in the Harris family. And he warned me not to be hasty. If he finds out the truth, he'll worry and fuss and stew. That's not good for his heart. It might kill him. Oh, how did I get myself into this mess?

SkiBum: What you need is rent-a-husband.

SkiBum: ;-)

MtnMama: Ha! You applying for the position, Joe?

SkiBum: Six weeks pretending to be your husband? Sounds like pretty gruesome work to me.

MtnMama: So much for the rent-a-husband idea. I think I need a good cry. Ought to last about a week.

SkiBum: Hey! Don't cry. It wouldn't be *that* gruesome. As I recall, you were a pretty cute ten-year-old. I suppose I could stomach it if I had to.

            - - -

SkiBum: MtnMama?

            - - -

SkiBum: Alicia? Are you still in the room?

            - - -

SkiBum: Hello?

MtnMama: I'm here. I was just thinking about what you said. Maybe this could work.

SkiBum: What could work?

MtnMama: You pretending to be my husband for a
           few weeks. Just while Grandpa is here.
           Maybe it's the perfect solution. You want
           to move back to Idaho, and you'll need
           to find a position. That takes time, espe-
           cially during the holidays. This would
           give you somewhere to stay until the new
           year. By then, you'd be employed and
           have a place of your own.

SkiBum: I hope you're not serious.

MtnMama: But I *am* serious. Not just serious. Des-
           perate!

                - - -

MtnMama: Joe?

SkiBum: My turn to think.

MtnMama: Will you do it?

                - - -

MtnMama: Joe?

SkiBum: Tell you what. I'm flying up next week
           anyway. We'll meet and talk while I'm in
           town. Then if you still want to go through
           with this crazy idea of yours, I'll consider
           it. But no promises.

MtnMama: It was *your* crazy idea.

SkiBum: I know. But I was kidding.

Chapter One

The streets of downtown Boise were busy on this second Saturday in November. People walked briskly along the sidewalks, their coat collars turned up and their heads leaning into the wind as they hurried from store to store. Shops and restaurants were crowded. A good sign for retailers, since the Christmas shopping season hadn't yet begun in earnest.

Alicia Harris sat at a table in Espresso Heaven, a coffee shop on Main Street, waiting anxiously for someone who looked like Joe Palermo—thirty-six years old, six foot two, black hair, brown eyes—to walk through the door. It wasn't much of a description, but it was all he'd given her. She doubted it mattered. She was certain she would recognize him, even after all these years.

No, it wasn't the description—or lack thereof—that

was making her anxious. It was wondering whether or not he would agree to her outlandish suggestion. If he didn't...

"Care for some coffee while you wait?" the waitress asked, drawing Alicia's gaze from the street scene.

"No, thanks. But I would like some herbal tea, if you have any."

"Sure thing. Whole selection. Be right back."

Alicia laid a hand on her extended abdomen. "Maybe this *is* a crazy idea, Humphrey." Humphrey was her pet name for her unborn child. "He *could* be an ax murderer."

Joe had suggested that possibility last night when they'd spoken by phone. He'd called from the motel near the airport shortly after checking in.

"You're taking quite a risk, Alicia," he'd said. "You don't know much about me really. Just old memories and some live chats on the Internet. I could be criminally insane. I could be an ax murderer."

She didn't believe he was dangerous, of course. She'd known the entire Palermo family when she was a girl, had made mud pies in the backyard with Joe's younger sister, Belinda. In fact, she'd had a major crush on "Joey" when she was ten and he was seventeen. But the Palermos had moved to California before she could grow up and make him notice her.

No, Joe was no ax murderer. There were plenty of things she didn't know about him, nineteen years later, but she was certain the boy who used to fix her bicycle chains and search for her missing cat was no monster.

A blast of cold air signaled the opening of the coffee shop's door. Alicia glanced up…and stopped breathing.

She was over seven months pregnant and already as big as a barn. She hadn't had a good hair day in at least fifteen weeks. Before leaving the house, she'd hidden the mess under a black and red Cat-in-the-Hat-type knitted cap. It probably didn't look much better than her hair. To top it all off, three pimples had appeared on her forehead this morning and now glowed as bright and red as Rudolph's nose.

And then there was Joe Palermo.

How did an Adonis at seventeen become even more handsome nearly two decades later? Shouldn't he have wrinkles or a receding hairline or a middle-age paunch or something?

He found her with his eyes, and he smiled.

Good grief! They could light the Capitol Christmas tree with that smile.

She swallowed hard, then smiled in return, watching as he made his way toward her.

Get a grip, MtnMama. It's only SkiBum, and he's just here to consider doing you a favor. It doesn't matter how good-looking he is. He's still a man, and right now that makes him *verboten*. Off-limits.

He stopped on the opposite side of the table. "You must be Alicia." His gaze dropped to her abdomen. "Although you look a little different from the last time I saw you." He glanced up. "You're taller, right?"

"Right." She chuckled nervously.

"It's good to see you again, Alicia."

"You, too, Joe."

He pulled out the chair and slid onto the seat. The

waitress appeared before he had time to remove his coat.

"Can I get you something?" she asked, sounding breathless.

"Large coffee. Black. Thanks."

"No frills," Alicia said as the waitress hurried away, obviously eager to fill the order and return as quickly as possible.

He smiled again. "No frills."

Now she could see she'd been wrong. He *did* have a few wrinkles. Tiny smile lines around his eyes and the corners of his mouth. And darned attractive they were, too.

Oh, her wacky pregnant-hormones were doing a major number on her. She hadn't given a man the time of day since Grant walked out three weeks after their wedding. She wasn't going to start now. Playing the fool once per decade was her limit.

"Popular place," Joe said, intruding on her thoughts.

"Yes. I usually come about nine in the morning, before I open my store. It's a little more quiet in here then. The eight-to-fivers have come and gone, and I can sit in the corner and sip my tea while reading the paper."

The waitress arrived with Joe's coffee.

"Thanks," he said as he flashed the young woman one of his million-watt smiles. Then he looked at Alicia, giving the waitress no excuse to linger. "Okay, let's talk about why I'm here."

"No-nonsense. Is that the attorney in you?"

"I guess so."

She sat up a little straighter, drew a deep breath

and let it out. "Joe, I know this is a huge favor to ask of anyone. Especially since you haven't seen me in years. If there was someone else I could ask..." She sighed. "But there isn't."

"Do you really think it's the best way? I remember your grandfather, and he didn't strike me as—"

"I can't tell him the truth. If you'd seen him in the hospital as I did, you wouldn't ask me to. If he knew I was about to become a single mom, he'd worry about me, and worry is the last thing he needs to do."

A thoughtful frown drew Joe's thick, black eyebrows close together. "Deceit is rarely the best path to take."

"Is it so terrible to want to protect someone you love?"

"No," he answered softly. "It isn't terrible. Misguided, maybe, but not terrible."

Alicia looked out the window at the scurrying Saturday shoppers. "I never meant for things to get out of hand. I never meant to tell even the first lie. It just sort of...*happened.* It's a long, stupid story."

Joe had come to the café to tell Alicia he couldn't agree to this charade. He'd come to tell her there was no way, not even for a recently rediscovered childhood friend, he could pretend to be anybody's husband. After all, his opinion of marriage wasn't a particularly high one.

But there was something about Alicia...

Despite himself, he said, "Why don't you tell me a little more about—" he motioned toward her stomach "—all this? You've never gone into detail in the chat room."

"As if I'd want to risk the entire Internet knowing what an idiot I was." Still staring toward the window, she released a deep sigh. "It's bad enough my friends and employees know."

"*I'm* your friend, Alicia. You can tell me."

That drew her gaze back to him.

"Hormones," she whispered with a pitiful wave of her hand toward her tear-filled eyes. Then she grabbed her purse, opened it, and withdrew a packet of tissues. "Sorry."

"No problem." He sipped his coffee, waiting patiently.

After a lengthy silence, she began speaking in a low voice, so low Joe had to lean forward in his chair in order to hear her.

"I met Grant Reeves last March at a party. He was an acquaintance of one of my employees and was in town for a few weeks. He was from Reno where he worked as a carpenter. Grant was utterly charming, totally charismatic. He had a certain way about him that made all the women take notice. But it was me he paid special attention to that night. And every night after that, too. He wined and dined me, showered me with flowers and gifts. Nothing like it had happened to me before. I fell hard. He asked me to marry him two weeks later. He wanted to get married right away."

Joe whistled softly, which drew a wry look and a nod from Alicia.

"I called Grandpa Roger. He's the only family I've got left since my parents died, so he was naturally the first person I wanted to tell. I was excited and happy. I thought he'd be happy for me, too. But he warned me not to rush into anything. He said I should wait a while. He said if it was really love we felt for one another, then it would still be love in a few more weeks or months." She wiped her eyes with the tissue. "I was so angry at him. I said some very unkind things before hanging up the phone. I didn't listen to his advice either. Grant and I were married four days later."

Marry in haste, Joe mentally recited, and repent at leisure. Of course, *he* would've rewritten the old adage: Marry and repent. Period.

"I knew it was a mistake almost from the first day," she continued, "but I wouldn't have admitted it to anyone. My pride was involved by that time. I kept telling myself things would improve. We just had to get used to living together, to each other's idiosyncrasies. I tried not to complain that he was spending too much money and that he came home late so often."

Alicia fell silent. She worried her lower lip with her teeth while staring down at her hands, folded upon the table. Unshed tears swam before her blue-green eyes. She looked incredibly fragile and vulnerable.

All of Joe's protective instincts flared to life. But those instincts weren't good ones, he reminded himself. Better to ignore them.

He took another sip of his lukewarm coffee.

"I found Grant with another woman three weeks after we were married. He seemed surprised I was upset by it. Apparently we had very different ideas of what marriage meant."

"Apparently."

She took a quick breath and let it out. "We got a

divorce in Nevada. It only took a few weeks, since Grant was still a resident. It was all relatively painless and civilized. I was relieved I hadn't told Grandpa I'd gotten married.'' She sighed again.

Joe wondered if she realized how often she did that. The deep breath and audible sigh. The rise and fall of her shoulders. The worrying of her lower lip between her teeth.

''And then I discovered I was pregnant,'' she added softly.

''Did you tell Grant?''

''Yes. He said I'd have to prove it was his and accused me of marrying him for child support.'' She released a self-deprecating laugh. ''*This* after he nearly cleaned out my savings account in three weeks' time.''

If Grant Reeves had lived within a hundred miles of this coffee shop, Joe would have sought him out and taught that charming, charismatic son of a gun a thing or two.

With his fists.

''I told him I didn't want anything from him, not even his name on the birth certificate.'' She sat a little straighter, lifting her chin, a spark of determination in her eyes that hadn't been there a moment before. ''I have my own retail business, and it's doing well. I can support my baby without any help from him.''

''But…''

''But—'' her shoulders slumped again ''—there's my grandpa.''

''Why didn't you tell him the whole truth after you discovered you were pregnant?''

''I was going to. I was waiting for the right moment. A time when the truth wasn't going to make me look like an idiot.''

"You're not an idiot."

"No. But I felt like one. Anyway, I knew I couldn't keep putting things off. I mean, he was going to know *something* when I went to Arizona for a visit and had a baby with me.'' She smiled wryly. "Grandpa isn't senile."

Joe returned her smile.

"He had his heart attack before I could tell him." Her expression sobered. "I rushed down to Arizona to be with him. No one thought he was going to live. Not his doctors. Not his friends. No one. I couldn't very well tell him then."

"And he didn't *notice* you were pregnant?" He couldn't keep the skeptical note out of his voice.

"He was too sick to notice. I was careful how I dressed. Besides, I wasn't very big at the time." She glanced down. "Not like now." She placed both of her hands on her abdomen. "And Humphrey's still got two months to grow."

"Humphrey?"

"That's what I call him. Or her."

"You don't know the sex?"

"I didn't want to. I'd rather be surprised."

He could have told her she sounded as old-fashioned as she thought her grandfather.

She raised her eyes again. "So...here I am. I didn't tell Grandpa Roger I was married, let alone divorced, because I didn't want him to be disappointed in me. I can't tell him I'm pregnant and alone, because I don't want to worry him and put stress on his weak heart. And now he's coming for an extended holiday visit, and I need a husband.'' Her expression was full of hope. ''Just for pretend. Just for the holidays. I need him to think I've got someone to love and care for me after he's gone.''

Turn her down, Palermo. You don't need this sort of headache.

''Please, Joe.''

It would be the craziest thing he'd ever done.

''It's only for five and a half weeks.'' Her voice dropped to a whisper. ''Please.''

Undeniably, certifiably insane.

''All right, Alicia. I'll do it.''

Chapter Two

Eight days later, at ten minutes after three on a Sunday afternoon, Joe steered his sports utility vehicle off the freeway. Every spare inch of the SUV was packed with his possessions. What he hadn't been able to bring with him from California would be shipped later, after he got a place of his own. For now, it was in storage.

He pulled into the parking lot of a convenience store, then reached for his cell phone, flipped it open and dialed Alicia's number. She answered on the third ring.

"It's Joe," he said after her greeting. "I'm in Meridian. Care to give me directions to your place again?"

She did so.

"Sounds easy enough. I ought to be there in about ten, fifteen minutes. If I get lost, I'll call again."

"I'll be watching for you."

"See you soon." He flipped the phone closed.

Undeniably, certifiably insane.

During the past eight days, he'd analyzed why he'd agreed to this scheme. He'd considered every possible reason. The first reason was always the same: Alicia Harris was cute. Cute wasn't a word he'd normally use to describe a pregnant woman, but it did fit her, even in the ridiculous red-and-black hat she'd worn last week.

But cute wasn't a good enough reason to pretend to be her husband for the next five and a half weeks. Thus, he could only conclude insanity was the reason for his acquiescence.

With a shake of his head, he pulled out of the parking lot and drove south.

The farmland that had once surrounded tiny Meridian, Idaho had been consumed by urban sprawl. Joe had grown used to that in Southern California, but he hadn't expected it here. Not this much.

He took a couple of wrong turns, but eventually he found the big old farmhouse with its screened front porch and half a dozen sixty-feet-tall trees standing like naked sentinels on all sides. Despite its age, the house looked well cared for.

He turned his vehicle into the drive and shut off the engine.

Undeniably, certifiably insane.

Taking a deep breath, he opened the car door and stepped out. About the same time, the screen door to the porch screeched a warning, and Alicia came into view. She smiled, waving a greeting with her right hand. He waved back, then grabbed his duffel bag off the car seat and headed toward the house.

"You found me," she said.

Her short-cropped light-brown hair looked as if she'd raked her fingers through it moments before; it stuck out in all directions. She wore an oversize sweater that had lost whatever shape it once had, baggy gray sweatpants, and fuzzy pink bunny slippers, complete with floppy ears.

And he'd be darned if she didn't look even cuter than last week.

"I found you," he replied.

"Come in." She held the door open wider. "I was about to have some herbal tea. Or I've got orange soda and root beer in the fridge, if you prefer, or I can make coffee."

"Tea's fine, but I prefer the regular stuff if you've got it."

"I've got it."

He followed her through a large living area with hardwood floors and an eclectic collection of furniture, including an upright piano and a bronze sculpture of a horse and rider that was reminiscent of a Remington.

The kitchen had the same high ceiling as the living room, but it was cheerier due to large windows framed by lacy curtains instead of heavy brocade drapes, and yellow paint on the walls and cabinets instead of dark paneling and wallpaper. The kitchen was filled with homey little touches, the likes of which Joe hadn't seen since he'd watched *Happy Days* back in the seventies.

Alicia motioned toward a Formica and chrome table against the far wall. "Have a seat." Then she turned to the stove, lifted a copper teakettle from the back burner and filled two mugs with steaming water.

"How long have you lived here?" Joe asked as he settled onto one of the vinyl-upholstered chairs.

"Since the summer after I graduated from high school."

"You were able to *buy* a house when you were eighteen?"

She smiled. "Of course not. It was my grandparents'. When Grandpa Roger retired and they relocated to Arizona, they gave this place to me. I had about eight roommates living with me during my college years. It helped pay the power bill." She set his mug on the table, then sat on the chair opposite him.

"You never wanted to leave Idaho?" he asked.

"What for? Everything I want is here."

"Guess I can't argue with that or I wouldn't be back myself." He lifted his mug and took a sip.

That was the precise moment the chair viciously attacked his right leg.

The instant Joe vaulted out of his chair with a yowl, his mug clattering to the floor, spilling tea everywhere, Alicia knew what had happened.

"Rosie!" she scolded, leaning down—not an easy thing to do these days—to peer under the table.

The orange tabby cat sat in the corner, looking quite pleased with herself.

"Rosie?" Joe followed Alicia's example, bending over to see his assailant for himself.

Alicia shook her finger. "Shame on you, Rosie Harris."

The cat looked at Joe and hissed.

"What sort of demon is that?"

"She's not a demon. Strangers make her nervous."

Joe straightened. "They make *her* nervous? *She's* the one with the claws."

Alicia sat up. "She'll be okay once she gets used to you."

"She'd better." He scowled. "Got a mop? I'll clean up this mess."

"I'll do it. She's my cat." She started to rise, but he stopped her with a hand on her shoulder.

"No, I'll do it. Just tell me where the mop is."

"In the utility room."

"Any more cats lying in wait to take pieces out of me?"

She shook her head. "No more cats. But there's an overly friendly sheepdog in the backyard. I'll introduce you to Rags later."

"Great," he muttered as he turned away. "Just great."

Alicia bit her lip to keep from laughing out loud.

"Go ahead," he said without looking at her. "Laugh all you want. What goes around comes around."

"So I've heard."

Joe knew there was a good reason he'd lived the past two decades without owning a pet. With his left hand grasping the mop handle, he leaned down to check his right calf. He wouldn't be surprised if he found it bleeding. It wasn't, but there were a couple of thin red welts.

"This could be a visit to purgatory," he said to himself.

It wasn't too late, of course. He could tell Alicia

he'd changed his mind. He could get a room at a hotel and settle in until he got something more permanent. Nothing irreversible had happened yet.

He opened the utility room door and stopped still, captured by the view before him.

Alicia leaned back in one of those ugly fifties chairs that looked as if they were straight out of a trolley car diner. She stroked her belly with both hands, a tender smile curving her bow-like mouth.

"Humphrey," she said softly, "you're gonna have to help teach Rosie some manners when you get here. I don't seem to be doing much of a job of it."

Humphrey. What kind of name was that to call a kid? The baby was likely to be born with a textbook full of classic neuroses. It would take years of counseling to straighten him out. Joe doubted Alicia's insurance plan would cover the fees of those expensive shrinks.

As if she'd felt his gaze upon her, she glanced his way. Her smile vanished.

He was sorry to see it go. "Found it." He held up the mop. "Is it safe to come out?"

It worked. She smiled again. "Yes. Rosie's gone."

"You sure?" He poked his head around the edge of the door, pretending to be nervous.

"I'm sure." She pushed up from her chair. "While you do that, I'll make sure everything's ready for you in the guest room."

"Hey, Alicia."

She stopped and looked over her shoulder.

"Where am I going to sleep while your grandfather's here? In the guest room?"

"Of course not." She turned toward him, her eyes widening. "I guess I forgot to think about that."

"Maybe you'd better." He halfway expected her to admit defeat.

She didn't. "I know. There's an old sofa bed on the back porch. We'll move it into my bedroom, and you can sleep there. Grandpa Roger won't know the difference. Not if we keep the door closed."

So much for his expectations.

"Joe? Are you trying to back out?"

As everyone in the world knew—judging by the countless jokes he'd heard over the past decade—lawyers were cold, calculating scavengers, the bottom feeders of society, out to cut whoever's throat they must. But Joe didn't feel cold or calculating when she looked at him with those large blue-green eyes of hers. Instead, he felt like some chivalrous knight riding out to protect the fair damsel in distress.

Which was about the most *absurd* thing he'd ever heard!

"No," he answered as he turned away and applied the mop to the floor with gusto. "I made a promise and I'll keep it. But I think this is all one big mistake."

Undeniably, certifiably insane.

They had three days to learn everything they could about each other. Alicia knew it wasn't much time.

"We must *seem* as though we're in love," she said as they sat down that evening to a supper of green salad, spaghetti and garlic bread. "If we've been married for nearly eight months, we should have some sort of routine worked out." She reached for the salt shaker. "So tell me. Are you a morning person or a night person?"

"Night."

"I love mornings. I'm all sunshine and singing."

"That's sick." He tore off a piece of garlic bread from the loaf. "My turn. Do you drink herbal tea because you like it or because you're pregnant?"

"Both. But normally I prefer coffee in the morning." She twirled spaghetti around her fork. "My doctor's name is Jamison. Matt Jamison. He's a general practitioner, and he's been my doctor for the past eight years."

"Why didn't you take my name when we got married? Are you a left-wing, male-bashing feminist type?"

She laughed. "Hardly. I'm politically a moderate. More conservative than liberal. But you have a good point. Grandpa Roger will ask that, too. About the name thing." She pondered the matter for a few moments while eating. "I suppose we could use the excuse of all the red tape the store would have to go through."

"What kind of store is it, by the way? What's the name?"

"It's called Bundles of Joy, and it's a maternity and baby shop."

Joe raised an eyebrow as he straightened in his chair. "You're kidding."

"No. It's true."

"How long have you been in business?"

"For five years. I moved the store to the Main Street location three years ago. It's one block from the coffee shop where we met last week." She frowned. "Didn't we cover any of this in the chat room when we first figured out we used to know each other?"

"Some. But we'd better go over it again and again."

Alicia had the sneaking suspicion Joe was beginning to enjoy himself. Perhaps this was a little like preparing for a trial. She could almost see the wheels in his head turning.

"What's the story about how we became reacquainted?" he asked. "And what are you telling your grandfather about why you kept the marriage a secret all this time?"

Her appetite, normally robust, was suddenly gone. She pushed her plate away, then slid her chair back from the table and rose. She walked over to the window. A nearly full moon was peeking over the mountains in the east. In a short while, it would be almost as bright as day outside.

She hated the idea of lying to Grandpa Roger. But what else could she do? He didn't need stress right now, not with his health so fragile. She remembered how he'd looked in that hospital room with machines beeping and fluids dripping through tubes. It was nothing short of a miracle that he was alive today, and he wasn't out of danger yet.

No, she didn't have any other choice. She would tell a thousand lies if she had to. She would pretend to be married and happy. To protect Grandpa Roger, she would do anything.

Joe touched her shoulder.

Surprised—she hadn't heard his approach—she turned quickly.

"You okay?" he asked, his voice gentle and low, his eyes watching her with concern.

She nodded, feeling dangerously weepy.

"Maybe we've covered enough for tonight. We can start again in the morning."

"Thanks for doing this, Joe." She swallowed the lump in her throat. "I can't say it enough. Thanks. I know it's an imposition."

He grinned. "I don't know. Free rent for six weeks. Somebody to talk to over a great supper of spaghetti. What's an imposition about that?"

"But it is, and we both know it."

"Hey." He leaned a little closer, laying the flat of his hand against her cheek. "What're old friends for?"

Her heart leaped in her chest. Her breath felt short.

Joe's eyes widened a fraction, then he stepped back from her. Looking over his shoulder toward the table, he said, "I'll clear up. You go on to bed."

"You don't have to—"

"I'm used to doing dishes, Alicia. I've been taking care of myself for a lot of years."

She should ask him about his brief marriage. It was something a second wife would know. But that could wait for another time.

"Go on." He jerked his head toward the doorway. "I know where the guest room and bath are. I'll make sure everything's locked up and the lights turned out." He smiled again. "See you in the morning."

She half wished he would take her in his arms. Then common sense returned.

"Good night," she whispered, then hurried out of the kitchen.

"That went well, Palermo," Joe muttered as soon as Alicia disappeared from view.

This knight-in-shining-armor gig wasn't as easy as it looked.

He cleared the table, setting dirty dishes on the counter and putting leftovers in the fridge. Then he filled the deep sink with hot sudsy water and washed the dishes, setting them in the drain to air dry.

All the while he was thinking about Alicia, her love for her grandfather, and what a predicament she was in because of some jerk named Grant. Of course, that part was her own fault. Nobody with a lick of sense got married just three weeks after meeting someone.

He thought of Marlene. His ex-wife. He and Marlene had known each other for four years before they got married, and their marriage hadn't lasted much longer than Alicia's. Only six months, but those had been the longest six months of Joe's life. Six months of hell on earth.

He winced. His ex-wife had taken him to the cleaners in their divorce. Joseph Palermo, hot-shot attorney, tops in his class...and major stooge.

One thing he'd learned from that decade-old experience. Marriage wasn't for him. He enjoyed the company of women as well as the next guy. But at the end of the day, he was perfectly content to return to a house of silence. Besides, like his dad before him, Joe worked most evenings and weekends. He loved being an attorney, and he became totally immersed in his cases. He didn't expect that to change just because he'd moved to Idaho to escape the southern California rat race. And what free time he found he meant to spend on the ski slopes or hiking the back country.

No, he wasn't—and wouldn't ever be—family man material.

He glanced around the bright yellow kitchen with all its cozy touches. Could he see himself living in a home like this?

Not hardly.

He hung up the dish towel, flicked off the light switch and headed for the guest room.

"Oh, Humphrey," Alicia whispered, "what's going on?"

Lying on her bed beneath her warm down comforter, she stared upward, watching as moonlight and shadows danced across her ceiling.

Rags whimpered and laid her head on the bed near Alicia's side. Alicia ruffled the Old English sheepdog's ears.

"How about you, girl? You have any ideas?"

The dog plopped both of her front paws on the bed and began wagging her tail.

"Okay. For a little while."

Rags jumped onto the mattress and plopped down next to her mistress.

Alicia didn't know whether to laugh or cry. There she was, big, pregnant, single, and in bed with her dog. And down the hall she could hear water running in the guest bathroom while Joe, one of the best-looking men she'd ever seen, got ready to retire for the night—in another room.

If that wasn't a commentary on her life, she didn't know what was.

Rags flopped her furry head onto Alicia's abdomen and whimpered again.

"My thoughts exactly," she whispered to the dog. "My thoughts exactly."

Chapter Three

Joe awakened to the scent of coffee percolating.

"Mmm."

Without opening his eyes, he tossed aside the blankets, felt with his toes for his slippers while at the same time reaching for his robe, which he'd left on the foot of the bed. A moment later he stood, eyes now half-open, his vision blurred with sleep.

He took a couple of steps toward the bedroom door...and stumbled over something large and immobile. He pitched headlong into the bureau before crashing to the floor.

Alternately groaning and muttering curses, he rolled onto his back...

And found himself staring into a furry face with a shiny black nose and open mouth full of teeth.

"What the—" He started to sit up.

A large paw landed on his chest, shoving him back to the floor.

"Alicia!"

The dog slapped his face with its sloppy-wet tongue.

"Alicia!"

She arrived a second or two later. "Oh, my goodness. Rags, get off him." She hurried into the room. "Rags, *go!*"

The instant the dog moved, Joe jumped up from the floor.

"Oh, I'm sorry." She choked on what sounded like a giggle, then tried to hide it by saying again, "I'm *so* sorry. I didn't know Rags was in here."

He rubbed his head, then checked his fingers for blood.

"I told you she's overly affectionate. She loves people."

Joe glared toward the open doorway. The dog was sitting in the hall, its head tipped to one side, its eyes obscured by that ridiculous mop of hair. Joe suspected the giant canine was grinning at him.

"She wouldn't hurt you," Alicia added. "Honest."

"Oh, really?" He turned his glare on her. "Want to feel the lump forming on my head as we speak?"

Her lips quivered, and the twinkle of amusement in her eyes was unmistakable.

"You think it's funny?"

"I'm sorry," she repeated. "It's just…it's just…" She covered her mouth with one hand. "If you could've seen the two of you as I did."

"Oh, yeah. A regular comedy team."

"I'm sorry."

"Okay. Enough with the apologies." He muttered a few more choice words under his breath, then added, "I need that coffee."

She stepped out of his way, allowing him to walk past her. She was wise enough not to follow immediately.

In the kitchen Joe found an oversize mug on the counter next to the coffeepot. He filled it to the brim, then turned and leaned against the counter while taking his first sip of the dark brew.

Ambrosia!

Alicia Harris knew how to make good coffee. That was some consolation.

He took another sip, then released a deep sigh.

"The way you like it?" she asked from the doorway.

"Yeah." He looked toward her. "It's good."

"You said you're not a morning person. Would you rather I left you alone?"

"Not much point in it now."

She gave him a tentative smile, and he suspected she was about to start apologizing again.

He spoke before she could. "What's on the agenda for today?"

"I thought I'd take you into the shop. Introduce you to my employees."

She was wearing those silly bunny slippers, along with a soft-ribbed bathrobe in the same shade of pink. Her hair had a mussed, just-got-up look about it. Darned cute, too.

The women Joe had dated over the past decade or so would rather die than be seen like this. If asked, he'd have said he preferred it that way. Now he wasn't so sure. There was something appealing about Alicia in that getup.

He gave his head a slight shake, as if denying the thought. "I assume your employees are among the few who know the truth."

"Yes. There wasn't any way around it."

He nodded.

"But I can trust them."

He chose not to explain how the risk of discovery grew with every person who knew. If they wanted to pull off this charade, they'd better keep Grandpa Roger as close to home as they could.

"I did decide what to tell my grandfather." Alicia raked the fingers of one hand through her already-tousled hair. "About why I've kept our marriage a secret. I'm going to say I was so angry after our fight that I didn't tell him out of spite. Then when he got sick, I decided to wait until he was better. And after he said he was coming for a visit, I simply waited to surprise him. I'll say I didn't want to give him any sudden shocks over the phone."

"Do you think he'll buy it? That's a mighty flimsy story."

"I know." Her shoulders slumped. "But I thought it was better to stick as close to the truth as possible."

"Did you ever mention Grant's name to him?"

"Yes. When I told him I was getting married. But that was months ago and only one conversation that ended badly. If he remembers, I'll say he misunderstood me."

"Grant Reeves. Joe Palermo. Oh, sure. I see how he could confuse the two."

She started to cry.

He felt like a heel.

"We...I...we...have to make...this work," she blubbered.

Joe set down his mug and went to her, gathered her into his arms and held her close. "I'm sorry." He stroked her hair. "I didn't mean to be sarcastic. Don't worry. We'll carry this off. I did theater in high school. Remember? You came with Belinda to one of my plays. I'll be a fine actor. Your grandpa will never suspect a thing."

Alicia allowed herself to sink into the safety of Joe's embrace. It felt good to lean on someone else. She was tired of being strong and courageous.

But self-indulgence was a momentary thing. She couldn't let it last.

She placed her palms against his chest and gently pushed herself away. "I seem to be crying all the time. I don't suppose you'd believe me if I swore this isn't normal." She wiped the tears from her cheeks.

"I guess I bring out the worst in you," he replied, his voice husky.

"No, I think we can blame this on Humphrey."

"Good ol' Humphrey."

She tried to smile, but the attempt was weak.

"Go wash your face." He motioned toward the hall. "I'll grab a bite to eat, then shower, and we can go into town."

She didn't argue. It was more prudent to beat a hasty retreat.

But retreating from whom?

Joe Palermo or herself?

"Wow!" Susie Notter, the assistant manager at Bundles of Joy, rolled her eyes at Alicia. "You gotta give me directions to one of those Internet chat rooms if *he's* an example of the kind of guy you find there.''

Alicia poked the young woman in the ribs with her elbow. ''Shh. He'll hear you.''

''Well, when you're through playing house with him,'' Susie whispered, ''you can tell Mr. Palermo I've got a spare room he's welcome to. And he won't even have to meet any of my family.''

A number of terse responses popped into Alicia's head. She bit her tongue to keep from saying any of them. It wasn't her place to decide what Joe would or wouldn't do after the holidays. And Susie was a nice person, a good friend. If Joe was looking for someone special in his life, Susie would fit the bill.

Joe turned from the wall of stuffed animals he'd been inspecting. He held up a furry seal. ''Looks like an appropriate toy for a kid called Humphrey. Don't you think?''

Her heart did a somersault, leaving her unable to speak. The best she could do was smile and nod in response.

''Does your husband get a store discount?'' he asked.

My husband...

Susie answered for her. ''Of course he does. Come over here, Mr. Palermo, and I'll ring up your purchase.''

Joe was just an old friend, Alicia reminded herself. Nothing more. She didn't want him to be anything more than that. Therefore, these feelings meant nothing.

She had to remember she'd fallen hard and fast for

Grant, and look where it got her. Not that she was sorry about having this baby, but she did regret the circumstances surrounding it. She believed in marriage for a lifetime, the Ward-and-June-Cleaver kind of household, two-point-three kids, the whole "American dream" bit.

She placed a hand on her abdomen. "Sorry, Humphrey," she said softly. "It would be nice to have a daddy, but we'll do the best we can on our own."

Joe turned from the cash register, purchase in hand. His grin was still in place, and it stole her breath away a second time.

"How about I take you to lunch?" he asked.

She doubted she could eat a bite.

"Okay," she answered.

He walked toward her, took hold of her arm, then glanced over his shoulder. "Nice to have met you, Susie." He looked in the other direction. "You, too, Judy," he said to the other salesperson.

With that, he guided Alicia toward the front door.

It took some doing, but Joe managed to shake Alicia free from whatever strange mood had overtaken her.

Over a lunch of clam chowder and corn bread, they reminisced about the old days when they'd been neighbors in a middle-class Meridian neighborhood. They laughed often, their conversation filled with the words *Do you remember...?* Alicia even confessed she'd had a crush on him when she was little and had wanted him to be the first boy to kiss her. He grinned when he heard it, liking the idea more than he should.

"Must have been fate we turned up in the Idaho

chat room at the same time," he said. "I didn't intend to strike up an on-line friendship. I just wanted information about Boise. And who would have thought I'd meet someone I knew as a kid?"

"It *was* unexpected, wasn't it? I'd only been in that chat room once before. I don't even know why I spoke up and answered your questions. I'm usually a lurker whenever I'm on the Net."

"I'm glad you didn't lurk that time."

"Me, too," she replied softly, smiling again.

"You know what surprises me most? You're not bitter about what happened to you. I mean, it could have soured you on all men the way your ex treated you."

Her smile faded. "All men didn't have anything to do with this. It was between me and Grant, and I was at fault, too." She tipped her head slightly to one side. "How about you? Did your ex-wife sour you on all women?"

"Maybe not on all women, but certainly on marriage. I don't intend to ever go that route again." He wished he'd never introduced the topic.

"You don't want to have children of your own?"

"No." He shook his head. "I wouldn't make a good father. I'm too much like my old man. He didn't have time for the kids he had. A workaholic shouldn't have children. It makes things tough on everyone involved."

"And you're a workaholic?"

"With a capital *W*."

"How very sad," she said in a low voice. Then, "Maybe we should go. I've got grocery shopping to do. I'm picking up the turkey today."

Wordlessly Joe rose, then stepped around the table to pull out her chair, offering his hand to help her to her feet. As she stood, her shoulder rubbed against his chest. He could smell her musky cologne. Her aquamarine eyes seemed darker than usual as she met his gaze. The restaurant sounds faded into the distance.

She wasn't ten, and he wouldn't be the first, but he wouldn't mind kissing her now.

Alicia blushed, as if she'd read his thoughts.

If he wasn't careful, Joe warned himself, he'd forget this was all pretend and he'd make an A-number-one fool out of himself.

He let go of her hand. "I'll pay the bill and meet you at the front door."

He walked away without a backward glance, hoping it wasn't already too late to avoid playing the fool.

By the time the two of them returned home, Alicia was exhausted. The grocery store had been jam-packed. It seemed she wasn't the only one who waited for Thanksgiving week to do her shopping. Big mistake. The lines had been long, the checkout clerks frazzled.

It didn't help that every time she looked at Joe she remembered the moment when she'd thought he might kiss her. Worse yet, she remembered wanting him to.

After he helped her carry the bags of groceries into the kitchen, Joe decided to move the sofa bed into the house from the back porch.

"It's awfully heavy," Alicia said. "You should have help."

"You can't be lifting and pushing."

"No, but I'm sure I could ask someone."

"I thought we agreed the fewer people who know about this the better."

"Yes, but—"

"No buts. Besides, I can manage."

She decided it was better not to argue the point. She would never win. She could tell by the set of his jaw.

It took a while, but Joe did manage to single-handedly—accompanied by plenty of grunting and muttering—move the sofa bed from the porch, through the kitchen, down the hall and into Alicia's bedroom. She tried once to help him, but her attempt was firmly rebuffed.

Before she could decide whether she felt pampered or was angered by his proprietary tone, the phone rang. She went to the kitchen to answer it.

"Hello, my girl," came the familiar voice from the other end of the wire.

"Grandpa? Is something wrong?"

"Does something have to be wrong for me to call you?"

"No. It's just, you'll be here in a couple of days, and I didn't expect—"

"Are you going to fuss over me like one of those confounded nurses the whole time I'm there?"

"Yes." She smiled tenderly, envisioning the elderly man with the perpetual twinkle in his eyes.

"Okay. Now that *that's* settled, the reason I called was to tell you my itinerary has changed. I'll be in an hour earlier on Wednesday. Nice surprise, isn't it?"

"Yes, it is."

Joe appeared in the doorway. The way he looked caused her heart to flutter.

"Grandpa, I've got a surprise for you myself." She glanced at her belly. "A couple of them actually."

"What?"

"I don't want to tell you over the phone. You'll have to wait until you get here."

"Teasing your grandpa, are you?"

"Maybe a little." She dropped her gaze to the floor. "I love you."

"I love you, too."

"I'm looking forward to your visit. Very much."

"Me, too. So I'll see you at the airport on Wednesday. One o'clock instead of two. Same flight number."

"I'll be there with bells on."

"Goodbye, dear. See you soon."

"Bye, Grandpa."

The connection was broken. Alicia hung up the phone.

"Everything okay?" Joe asked.

She turned toward him. "Yes." But the fluttering in her heart when she met his gaze made her wonder if she spoke the truth.

Chapter Four

Alicia was shaking. Whether from excitement or nerves, Joe couldn't be sure. He suspected it was a combination of the two.

As the first passengers exited the jetway, Joe placed an arm around her back and whispered, "Here we go, sweetheart."

She glanced up, obviously surprised by the endearment.

"The charade begins," he added quickly, wanting her to understand his choice of words was all part of the pretense. "Act 1, scene 1. Remember your lines?"

She gave him a pained smile, accompanied by a nod, then returned her gaze to the jetway.

The waiting area and concourse grew noisier as friends and family were welcomed.

"There he is!" Alicia raised an arm and waved. "Grandpa! Over here!"

Roger Harris hadn't changed much over the past two decades. Perhaps the good reverend was a bit thinner, but his hair was the same stone-gray and his smile was as warm and friendly as Joe remembered. In fact, he would say her grandfather looked pretty darn good for a man of seventy-seven in not the best of health.

There was a definite question in the elderly man's eyes as he approached the two of them. Then he stopped short, his eyes widening, and Joe knew Roger Harris had finally noticed Alicia's expanded waistline.

"Hi, Grandpa." Her greeting was tentative.

Joe tightened his arm and urged her forward with a gentle pressure.

"I assume *this*—" Grandpa Roger glanced at her belly "—is part of my surprise?"

"Yes." She took a deep breath. "And here is the other part. This is Joe Palermo. My husband."

Joe offered his hand. "Nice to meet you, sir."

Grandpa Roger hesitated only a moment before taking Joe's hand in his. "And you, young man." His gaze was as firm as his grasp. "Have we met before?"

"Years ago, Mr. Harris. When I was a kid. I lived across the street from Alicia until my dad transferred to California. I came back to Idaho recently to enjoy the simpler life."

Grandpa Roger nodded, then looked at his granddaughter once again. "I think it's time for a hug. The rest of the story can wait."

She responded immediately, throwing her arms

around him and holding on tight. Her grandfather said something to her, but he spoke too softly for Joe to understand. When the older man looked at him over Alicia's shoulder, Joe felt a sudden desire to earn his respect.

He wondered if that would be possible, given the lies he intended to tell.

It had been four years since Roger Harris's last visit to Idaho. As was always the case, he saw signs of change and growth during the drive from the airport to the old farmhouse he and his wife had lived in for the twenty-five years he'd pastored the small church in Meridian. He was sorry to see the farmland disappearing, but he'd lived long enough to know and accept that progress often meant unwanted change.

Alicia glanced over her shoulder as Joe drove his SUV onto the freeway exit ramp. "Do you need anything at the store before we go home?"

"Not a thing, my girl."

She smiled, then turned forward, her gaze pausing briefly upon her husband before returning to the road before them.

Roger looked at the back of Joe Palermo's head, wondering why Alicia had kept her marriage a secret all these months. He suspected, whatever she told him, he wouldn't be hearing the whole truth. Something was amiss. He just didn't know what.

But he was willing to wait and observe and listen. His age and profession had taught him patience.

While Joe carried her grandfather's luggage into the house, Alicia put the kettle on for tea.

"Are you hungry, Grandpa? It'll be an hour before dinner's ready."

"I'm not in any hurry," he answered. "But I would like to hear more about you and Joe."

She'd known she couldn't put off this discussion for long.

"Why did you keep the marriage a secret from me?"

She turned. Her grandfather was seated on one of the kitchen chairs, watching her with those kind, loving eyes of his. She hated herself for the lies she was about to tell him, even if it was for his own good.

He patted his hand on the table. "Come sit down. Come talk to me."

"Okay," she answered softly as she obeyed.

"Are you happy?"

"Yes." She smiled to prove it, but inside she was quivering.

"Then tell me."

"Remember our argument when I told you I was getting married after a whirlwind romance?"

He nodded.

"I was so angry, I decided not to tell you Joe and I got married, despite your advice to wait awhile. It was silly and petty of me, I know, but that was my reason for keeping it a secret." She looked down at her hands, unable to meet his gaze while she spun her tale of half-truths and outright lies. "When I discovered I was pregnant, I knew I had to tell you, but I kept putting it off because I was ashamed of the way I'd acted. Then you got sick and I couldn't tell you until you were better. And…well…here you are." She ended with a slight shrug.

"Here I am."

She looked up. "I'm sorry, Grandpa. I didn't mean for it to happen this way."

"But you *are* happy?"

"Yes, I'm happy."

"And the baby? When is it due?"

"January 20."

"My first great-grandchild. I wish your grandmother could have lived to see this."

Her heart tightened. "Me, too."

Joe entered the kitchen at that moment. He hesitated in the doorway, then strode across the room, coming to a stop behind Alicia's chair. He placed his hands on her shoulders, leaned down, and kissed the top of her head.

A shiver raced through her.

"I put the bags on the bed, sir, and hung your suit in the closet."

"Thank you." Her grandfather motioned to another chair. "No time like the present to get acquainted. I've forgotten if Alicia told me what you do for a living."

"I'm an attorney."

Alicia noticed how calm Joe looked and sounded. She wished she felt the same.

"What sort of law do you practice?"

"Corporate, mostly, but I do some trial work, too."

"What firm are you with?"

Alicia felt a stab of alarm. They hadn't discussed any of this.

Grandpa Roger shook his head. "It sounds like I'm interrogating you, doesn't it?"

"I don't mind, sir. And to answer your question,

I'm not with any local firm as yet. I'm wrapping up some things for clients in California while working out of the house. I may be settled into a new firm by January, but I'm not in any hurry. I wouldn't mind being at home when our baby arrives.''

Our baby... Alicia imagined him holding a newborn in his arms.

''It'd give us more time to bond. My father worked such long hours, I hardly knew him. I'd like things to be different with my kid.''

''Wonderful sentiment,'' her grandfather said. ''And with laptops, faxes and e-mail, I guess no one has to have an outside office these days.''

''No, sir. That's very true.''

The kettle began to whistle. Alicia rose from her chair, excusing herself with a mumbled apology, glad for a moment to collect her thoughts. The way Joe had talked about bonding with his child and how he hadn't known his own father had left her oddly disturbed. She'd found herself believing him, caught up in the fantasy they were spinning for her grandfather.

''Do you need any help, sweetheart?'' Joe asked, breaking her concentration.

She knew her cheeks were flushed as she turned. ''No, thanks. I've got it.'' She carried the teacups to the table and set one before her grandfather, the other before Joe.

''She's still trying to get me to drink this herbal stuff,'' Joe said with a chuckle as his gaze met hers. ''Even after all these months together, she hasn't given up.''

Dropping through a hole in the floor would have been a convenient escape. It didn't happen.

"Alicia's always been a headstrong girl," Grandpa Roger said. "Mind of her own. I suppose you know I advised her against marrying in such a hurry."

"Yes, sir. So I heard." Joe glanced at the older man. "I'd like you to know, right up front, that keeping the news about our wedding and the baby from you was her idea. Not mine. I told her it was better to tell the truth."

Alicia wanted to kick him.

All things considered, the evening went well.

Over a supper of grilled chicken breasts, mashed potatoes, and peas with carrots, Alicia asked her grandfather about his friends in Arizona, about the heart specialist's recommendations for his diet, about anything that would steer the conversation away from Joe and their "marriage."

It wasn't yet nine o'clock when Grandpa Roger announced it was time for him to turn in.

"Are you feeling all right?" she asked, suddenly anxious.

"A bit tired, is all. It's been a long day." He rose from the easy chair where he'd been sitting. "I'll see you both in the morning. Good night."

"Good night," Alicia and Joe said in unison.

She waited until she heard the bedroom door close before she asked, "Do you think he's really all right? I should have insisted he lie down when we first got home."

"Alicia…" Joe laid his hand on her shoulder. "Relax. He said he was just tired."

"I know, but—"

He squeezed her shoulder. "He's okay."

She looked at him. The hint of a smile curved his mouth, and his gaze was filled with tenderness. She hoped she wasn't going to start crying again. She was sick to death of her propensity for turning on the waterworks.

"Maybe I'd better go to bed, too." She stood. "I'll be up early to put the turkey in the oven."

"I'm going to watch a bit of television."

She nodded.

"I'll try not to wake you when I come to bed."

Her breath caught. How could she have forgotten, even for a short while, that Joe would be sharing her bedroom for the next five weeks?

"I'll make up the sofa," she said before hurrying away, grateful he didn't volunteer to help.

The master bedroom was large, and the sofa and her bed were on opposite sides of the room. The connecting bath had a lock on the door. Alicia didn't have to worry about privacy or propriety. There was no reason for her heart to be racing the way it was.

Within a short time, she had the sofa bed opened and made up. Then she brushed her teeth, washed her face, put on her nightgown and crawled into bed, the lights out. But sleep didn't come quickly as she'd hoped.

How could it, when she kept wondering how soon Joe would come to bed?

Joe flicked through the local channels but didn't find anything worth watching. In California, he'd had a satellite system, complete with more channels than he'd known what to do with. Alicia didn't even have basic cable.

Alicia…

He glanced toward the master bedroom. No light showed beneath the door. She must be in bed, but he'd bet money she wasn't asleep yet. She'd been stretched tight as a drum all day. He wished he knew how to make her relax.

But she wasn't his responsibility, he reminded himself. This whole charade was her problem. He would do his part as best he could, but he couldn't fix everything. He sure couldn't make her feel better about it.

"Never should've agreed to this," he muttered as he got to his feet, at the same time clicking off the TV with the remote control.

After checking the lock on the front door, he put out the last light and made his way to the master bedroom. He turned the knob and pushed the door open slowly. A nightlight's soft glow illuminated his way to the bathroom.

He was nearly there when he heard a warning hiss, followed by a throaty feline growl. He froze in midstep. Where was that darn cat? If Rosie took another hunk out of his skin, he was going to wring her neck.

"Rosie," Alicia whispered, "stop that."

Joe looked toward the big four-poster bed. "Tell me when it's safe to move."

"It's safe. She's up here with me."

"Don't know why you keep that animal around. She's hazardous."

Alicia laughed softly.

"Sure, you find it amusing. You're not in danger of losing a leg." He stepped through the bathroom doorway. "Somebody ought to run over her with a truck."

Alicia watched as Joe pulled the bathroom door closed behind him, listened to the water running in the sink. "He didn't mean it, Rosie," she whispered. "But you really must stop hissing and swiping at him."

The cat purred in contentment, as docile and loving as you please.

"He's been an awfully good sport about this. So help me out." She rubbed the cat's exposed belly. "Behave yourself around him."

Alicia rolled onto her left side, her back toward the bathroom door. A short while later the water stopped running. The door opened. A few moments more and the sofa springs squeaked as Joe got settled for the night.

She wondered if he could hear the crazy patter of her heart.

He sighed. The springs squeaked again.

"I hope you don't find the mattress too uncomfortable," she whispered.

"Don't worry about me. I can sleep anywhere."

She wished she could say the same.

She was still wishing it an hour later as she listened to his steady breathing, a sound that seemed much too intimate for her own peace of mind.

Chapter Five

Joe was surprised to find daylight streaming through the windows when he opened his eyes again. He glanced toward the bed, thinking Alicia must have overslept, but she wasn't there. He sat up, at the same time raking his fingers through his hair and yawning. He'd slept like a log. Best night's sleep he'd had since he got here.

Through the closed bedroom door, he heard voices. Alicia's grandfather must be up, too, he thought as he tossed aside the blankets and sheet.

He started to lower his feet to the floor, then remembered Rosie.

"Oh, no, you don't," he muttered as he leaned over, checking beneath the sofa bed. "You're not getting another piece of me."

The feline wasn't hiding there.

Satisfied he was safe, he got out of bed. He removed the sheets and blankets, folding them before placing them and the pillows in a corner out of view of the doorway. Then he closed the sofa and returned the cushions to their proper place. Satisfied there were no lingering signs of his true sleeping arrangements, he grabbed his clothes and went into the bathroom.

Twenty minutes later, freshly showered and shaved, he entered the kitchen. Alicia and her grandfather were seated at the table.

"Good morning," he said as he walked across the room, pausing beside Alicia's chair. He leaned down and kissed the back of her neck. "Sorry. I overslept. I meant to help you with the turkey."

"It's okay." She didn't quite meet his gaze. "I could see you were tired." Her cheeks were flushed.

Joe looked toward her grandfather. "Good morning, sir. Did you sleep well?"

"I certainly did. That's a comfortable bed in the guest room."

"Yes, it is."

Alicia shot him a warning glance.

Joe covered his blunder with a grin. "I need coffee. I can't think straight in the mornings without it." He turned and headed for the coffee maker.

"Alicia just told me about your wedding photos," Grandpa Roger said. "What a shame."

Our wedding photos? Joe thought, glad his back was turned to the older man. What wedding photos?

"The photographer assured us film doesn't get lost very often," Alicia said quickly. "We happened to be that rare occasion."

Joe breathed a silent sigh of relief, then faced the

others. "I was upset, but what could we do? He gave us our deposit back. It wasn't his fault."

"I think you should get new photos taken," Grandpa Roger said. "You'll want them for your children someday."

"It's a little late now." Alicia laid her hands on her abdomen. "I've outgrown my dress."

Joe took a sip of coffee before saying, "Maybe your grandfather's right. We should have some photos of us."

The glare she gave him could have caused a nuclear meltdown.

"Wonderful." Grandpa Roger slid his chair back from the table. "You can give me a five-by-seven for my Christmas present." He rose to his feet, picked up his breakfast dishes and carried them to the sink. "I'd better take my walk before the day gets away from me."

"Do you mind company?" Joe asked. "I could use some fresh air to wake me up."

"I'd be delighted, son. I'll get my coat."

"Are you crazy?" Alicia asked in a whisper the instant her grandfather was out of hearing. "Why did you volunteer to go with him? He'll end up asking you more questions."

"It can't be avoided. Might as well get used to it."

She knew he was right. But to volunteer…

"It'll look more suspicious if I avoid him."

"Okay. Just don't stay out too long. And for Pete's sake, keep your stories straight."

He grinned, and for a moment she thought he might give her a peck on the cheek.

But he didn't. He simply turned and strode out of the kitchen.

"It's a fine kettle of fish I've gotten myself into, Humphrey."

Shaking her head, she crossed to the refrigerator where she retrieved packages of carrots and celery. She hoped staying busy would keep her mind off all the things that could go wrong.

The sky was one of those crystal-clear winter-blues that almost hurts the eyes. The temperature hovered around freezing, and the two men could see their breath as they ambled down the quiet country road. The Boise mountains to the north and the Owyhee Mountains to the south wore cloaks of white, and despite the cloudless day, there seemed to be a promise of snowfall in the air.

"I miss winter, living in Arizona," Grandpa Roger said, breaking the self-imposed silence that had stretched between them.

"That's how I felt about California. I mean, all that sunshine's great for the sun worshipers, but that was never my scene. Give me the slopes any day of the week."

Alicia's grandfather glanced at Joe. "Alicia never cared much for skiing. Think she'll take it up now?"

"I don't know." He made a mental note to ask her. "But I'll do my best to change her mind."

"Well, it won't be this year."

"No, sir. It won't."

They continued in silence a short while longer.

"Joe?"

"Yes, sir?"

"Except for you now, I'm all the family Alicia's got. While I hope the good Lord will give me plenty more years on this earth, I'd like to know she's in good hands if I'm called home anytime soon."

"You can depend on me to take care of her, sir." He hadn't expected the lie to come so hard. "I'll see she doesn't go in want of anything." Maybe it didn't have to be a lie. Just because he wasn't married to Alicia Harris didn't mean he couldn't check on her every now and again, make certain she was okay.

The elderly man smiled. "Why don't you call me Roger or Grandpa? There shouldn't be all this formality between us, now that you and I are family. Especially not when you're about to make me a great-grandfather."

"No, sir," Joe answered automatically.

Grandpa Roger chuckled.

Joe grinned. "Sorry."

Another stretch of silence followed. Joe was surprised by how comfortable it felt. As if he and the older man had spent many such hours together.

"Tell me more about how you and Alicia became reacquainted. I know nothing about the Internet and how those chat rooms work. It's always seemed rather mysterious to me when I hear about it on the news."

"Nothing mysterious about it, sir."

Grandpa Roger raised an eyebrow.

Joe shrugged and continued. "It would be easier to show you than try to explain. Are you game?"

"I may be an old dog," he replied, "but I'm still able to learn a few new tricks. I'm willing if you are."

"Terrific. I'll set up my laptop when we get home."

* * *

Alicia stepped to the front room windows and looked outside. Relief flooded through her when she saw Grandpa Roger and Joe coming up the walk. They both looked calm and comfortable. Apparently there'd been no slipup on Joe's part.

She opened the door as they ascended the porch steps. "Are you frozen yet?"

"Not at all," her grandfather replied. "It's a lovely morning."

"Brr." She shuddered. "Too cold for my blood."

Joe stopped in front of her and casually kissed her cheek. Her heart missed a beat, and her breath caught in her chest.

"Did I say how pretty you look this morning?" he whispered. "I expect this is going to be the best Thanksgiving I've ever had."

A pleasant warmth surged through her veins.

A half second later she realized her grandfather was watching them and grinning from ear to ear. Of course. Joe was doing this for Grandpa Roger's benefit. She'd almost forgotten it was an act. For a moment she'd become a part of the fantasy.

"Do you need any help in the kitchen?" Joe continued.

She shook her head, her mouth too dry to speak.

"Good. I promised your grandfather I'd give him a lesson on the Internet." He smiled that sexy smile of his. "He hopes he can meet someone as pretty as you in a chat room."

Joe gave her another kiss, this time on the forehead. Then he strode toward the bedroom, whistling softly under his breath.

She stood beside the open door a moment or two longer, thankful for the cool air on her skin. Her head told her his words were nothing more than lines, but her heart longed to believe they were true.

She was embarrassed to admit, even to herself, how ridiculously hungry for a man's compliments she was.

Hormones again, she decided as she closed the door. Just these stupid hormones.

"Hey, Alicia," Joe called from the bedroom. "Can you come here a minute?"

"Coming." She headed for the hallway. "I'll be right back, Grandpa."

When she entered the master bedroom, she found Joe on his knees beside the sofa bed, looking beneath it.

"Lose something?" she asked.

"Yeah. My favorite pen. I keep it in the side pocket of my briefcase. I used it yesterday morning, but it isn't there now. Must've fallen out when I moved my stuff in here." He straightened, sitting back on his heels. "It's a marbled navy-blue color with a gold band. About this wide." He indicated the width with his right thumb and index finger. "Have you seen it?"

She shook her head. "Sorry."

A tiny frown furrowed his forehead. "Can't figure that out," he said softly to himself. Then he shrugged and rose from the floor. "I suppose it will turn up." He grabbed the case holding his laptop. "My new office is a bit crowded," he said, referring to the small room in the basement where his fax machine and files had been placed. "Is there another spot your grandfather and I can use?"

"There's a phone jack near the piano. That would work. The light's good, and the chairs are comfy."

"Okay." He stepped toward her, then stopped, his eyes locked with hers. "How come you don't like to snow ski?"

"What?"

"Your grandfather says you don't like to ski."

"No, I don't."

"Why?"

His eyes were the most luscious shade of brown. When he looked at her, so intent and earnest, she could hardly think straight.

"Alicia?"

She swallowed. "I didn't care for it, the times I've tried."

"Maybe you had the wrong instructor." He smiled as he tipped his head slightly to one side. "Do you suppose you'd give it another try for your husband?"

There went her heart, thumping erratically again.

"After the baby comes, of course," Joe went on.

He didn't have a clue how his words affected her. How could he? She wasn't sure *she* understood.

"But that's only…" He paused. "What? Less than eight weeks now?"

Somehow she found her voice. "I'm sure the season will be nearly over before the doctor would release me to go skiing."

"I know that." He lowered his voice. "But your grandfather was wondering if you might take it up now that we're married, and I thought I'd better find out. Seems like something we would've talked about. Doesn't it?"

He had a way of bursting her bubbles before she

got too carried away. She supposed she should be grateful for that.

"You're right," she answered. "We should have talked about it. And the answer is, no. I don't want to take up skiing."

"Too bad." He looked genuinely disappointed. "I think you could've learned to like it."

She had the horrible feeling he was right. She thought she could learn to like anything he wanted to teach her.

"I'd better baste the turkey," she whispered, hurrying away before those sharp eyes of his saw more than she wanted them to.

Joe frowned as he set his laptop on a table and connected a cord to the modem. What had gotten into him? Had he forgotten this was all an elaborate masquerade? He'd actually hoped Alicia would agree to go skiing with him sometime in the future. He'd actually been sorry when she refused him.

Too much time on my hands, he thought as he turned on the computer and watched it power up. "Time I got back to work."

"What's that?"

Joe looked over his shoulder at Alicia's grandfather. "Nothing. Just talking to myself."

"That's a sign of old age," Grandpa Roger said with a twinkle in his eyes.

"No doubt." He motioned to a chair. "Ready to begin?"

"I'm ready." The older man sat down.

"Great."

After about half an hour of preliminary computer

and Internet instructions, Joe could see that this "old dog," as Grandpa Roger had called himself, was plenty quick enough to learn new tricks. He suspected it would take no time at all before the retired minister was an Internet expert.

Once they were on-line, Joe helped him find some sites of interest using a search engine.

"Fascinating," Grandpa Roger said. "I had no idea there was so much available."

"And multiplying daily."

"Do you mind if I continue to—what's the word?—*surf* for a while?"

"Not at all." Joe glanced toward the kitchen.

"Go ahead. See if she needs any help. I'll holler if I get into trouble."

Joe hadn't meant to give the impression he was thinking about Alicia—even though he had been. With a nod, he rose from his chair and walked away. At the kitchen doorway, he paused. She was standing near the sink, her hands folded atop her swollen belly, her expression wistful as she gazed out the window at the sunny day. She looked so…beautiful. So kissable. So feminine and warm and tender. So…

He felt a sudden—and totally unexpected—wave of passion wash over him.

He'd known coming here, agreeing to this charade, had been a crazy thing to do, but he'd never expected to find himself desiring a woman who was seven months pregnant with another man's child. There must be something wrong with him.

She turned her head and saw him standing there. She gave him a hesitant smile. "How's the lesson coming?"

"Fine. Your grandfather's got a quick mind."

"Uh-huh."

The need to take her in his arms, to kiss her—*really* kiss her—overwhelmed him.

She checked her wristwatch, then crossed the kitchen to the stove. Guessing her intent and wanting to be near, he followed her there.

"Let me do that for you," he said. "You shouldn't be lifting."

He drew on the oven mitts, removed the roasting pan from the oven, then tipped it slightly to one side so she could baste the bird.

"Thank you," she said without looking at him.

Tiny fishhook curls lay against her nape. If he were to kiss her there, her hair would be soft, the skin on her neck would be smooth. He was sure of it.

When she finished basting the big bird, she thanked Joe again, still without turning her gaze on him. He was glad she kept her eyes averted. He didn't want her to discover what he was thinking and feeling.

He suspected it would be a huge mistake if she ever did discover it.

Chapter Six

Alicia arrived at the store an hour before it opened Friday morning. Like most retail businesses, Bundles of Joy relied on the day after Thanksgiving to make a hefty contribution to the profit margin for the year. She knew the day would be a long one and had warned both Joe and her grandfather not to expect her until ten o'clock that night.

"You shouldn't be putting in those kind of hours in your condition," Grandpa Roger had told her.

But what could she do? This was her livelihood. She was the boss. She had to be there.

Besides, this was the night of their special Father's Sale. From six to nine, the only females allowed in the store would be Alicia and her staff. This was an evening designed for husbands and fathers to come in and find those special gifts for their wives and children. Alicia had come up with the idea three years ago, and it had been a huge hit. Now it was an expected annual tradition.

In the back room she hung up her coat, then put her cold turkey sandwich in the small refrigerator before filling the coffeepot with water. By the time the coffee was done percolating, Susie had arrived.

"How was your Thanksgiving?" Susie shed her parka and draped it over a hanger.

"Very nice. How about yours?"

"Filling. I almost had to roll myself here from the parking lot. I always eat way too much at these things."

Alicia grinned as she nodded in agreement.

"Your *husband* and grandfather getting along?" There was a mischievous gleam in Susie's eyes as she asked her question.

"Yes." Alicia envisioned the two men as they'd sat, side by side, last evening, continuing her grandfather's lessons on using the Internet. Two boys with their toys, she thought now. If things continued this way, they would be the best of friends in no time.

"So if they're getting along," Susie inquired, "why the frown?"

"Was I frowning?"

"You know it."

Alicia gave her head a tiny shake. "It isn't anything. I was just lost in thought."

"Hmm." Susie poured herself a cup of coffee. "Are you worried about what will happen today while you're gone? I mean, the two of them left to their own devices. Scary."

"No, I'm not worried." At least, she hadn't been until Susie suggested it.

What were Grandpa and Joe going to do while she was at work? Why hadn't she considered how often the two men would be together without her? She and Joe had covered a lot of territory, made up a lot of "facts," but there was no way she'd told him everything he should know. Their real history was only days long, not eight months.

Alicia groaned.

Susie was right. She *should* be worried.

The computer showroom was a madhouse.

Joe glanced sideways at Alicia's grandfather as the glass-and-chrome doors swung closed behind them. "Are you sure you want to do this today?"

"I'm sure."

"I'd be happy to pick one out and bring it home to you."

"Young man, I'm not about to spend my remaining years living in dread of another heart attack. I want to experience this for myself."

Alicia would kill Joe if anything happened to the old man, but he knew it was futile to try to change Grandpa Roger's mind. He'd already discovered where Alicia got her stubborn streak.

A salesman appeared before them. "Can I help you?"

"Yes," Joe answered. "We're looking for a laptop for my friend here."

"Right this way."

Joe motioned for Grandpa Roger to follow the salesman, then fell into step behind the older man.

Above the din of conversations, he could hear the salesman begin his pitch.

Alicia, I turned your grandfather into an Internet junkie in less than twenty-four hours. I hope you'll forgive me.

On the heels of that thought, he wondered how her day was going. Was Bundles of Joy as jam-packed with customers as this showroom? He didn't know whether to hope so or not. She'd looked tired this morning. He suspected she wasn't sleeping well.

I wonder if it has anything to do with me.

He silently laughed at himself. What an absurd, egotistical notion! Why should he cause her to lose sleep? They were nothing to each other but friends.

And I'm the friend who finds her sexy.

"Joe?"

At the sound of Grandpa Roger's voice, he dragged his thoughts to the present. "Yeah?"

"You're the expert. What do you think?"

"Sorry. About what?"

The salesman did everything but roll his eyes in exasperation, then began his spiel a second time, enumerating all the advantages of the laptops on display.

An hour later, the two men left the store, their purchase made. Roger Harris was the brand-new owner of a lightweight, high-speed, state-of-the-art laptop computer. His eyes twinkled like a kid's on Christmas morning, and there was a definite spring in his step as they walked toward Joe's SUV.

"Let me buy you lunch," the older man offered. "We can have leftovers for supper."

"Sounds good to me. Where to?"

"How about Gracie's?"

Joe closed his door and stuck the key in the ignition. "Where's that?"

Grandpa Roger lifted an eyebrow. "You've been married eight months, and Alicia's never taken you to Gracie's?"

"We don't eat out much," Joe bluffed.

"I guess not."

He started the engine. "You point the way. I'll get us there. Maybe we can beat the lunch crowd."

Gracie's was one of those home-style restaurants found in every small town in America. It was in a converted brick house, nestled a block away from Meridian's main drag. A handicapped ramp had been added to the front entrance, and the backyard had been turned into a black-topped parking lot. Two ancient maple trees, their branches stripped bare by winter, stood as sentries on either side of the driveway.

They were too late to beat the lunch crowd, Joe realized as he pulled his vehicle into the only available spot. Or maybe they were too early to avoid the breakfast crowd. He couldn't be sure.

"Alicia, her grandmother and I used to come here the first Saturday of every month for breakfast," Grandpa Roger said. "It was a favorite tradition. Gracie serves the best French toast with homemade maple syrup you've ever eaten."

Joe glanced at him. "Oh, yeah," he lied. "I think I remember her telling me about it." He got out of the vehicle before the older man could reply.

A change of topic was in order, he decided as the two of them walked toward the entrance. And after today, he planned to avoid this kind of thing like the plague. Ever since he'd sat in that Boise coffee shop two weeks ago and agreed to this crazy plan of Alicia's, he'd been doing things totally out of character. He'd better start acting like the work-obsessed attorney he was and forget this cozy-family make-believe world he'd been sucked into.

By the time he and Grandpa Roger were seated at a table near one of the gingham-curtained windows, Joe had managed to steer the conversation back to computers and the Internet. He succeeded in keeping it there until midway through the meal.

"I'm curious about something," Alicia's grandfather began.

Joe tried not to let his apprehension show.

"Doesn't it bother you that Alicia didn't change her last name to Palermo?"

"Well..." he said slowly, trying for just the right tone. "Maybe a little. But they do it a lot these days."

"It seems so unlike her. My granddaughter's always been a traditionalist. *And* a romantic." Grandpa Roger looked at Joe. "Only a romantic could fall in love and marry so quickly, right?"

"I guess so."

"Which means you must be a bit of a romantic yourself."

Joe Palermo? A romantic? When pigs fly.

He cleared his throat, then said, "We discussed it, of course. The name thing. It just made more sense, because of her business, to leave things as they were."

"I suppose." Grandpa Roger looked unconvinced. "Call me old-fashioned. I still think a man and wife should share the same last name with their children. The baby will be a Palermo, after all."

"Humphrey Palermo?" Joe said beneath his breath—and then grinned at the ridiculous sound of it.

"Pardon?"

His grin broadened. "Nothing, sir. Just a private joke between Alicia and me."

The older man smiled, too. "Every marriage should have a few of those. Keeps you close."

Joe felt a stab of guilt. He and Alicia had fabricated a life, and Roger Harris had bought into it, hook, line and sinker. When her grandfather looked at the two of them, he saw a couple of romantics in love. He couldn't know—and hopefully would never know—how wrong he was.

"This is our first," the man said as he perused the racks of maternity wear. "We've been trying for over ten years to have a baby and just about gave up hope." His gaze shifted to Alicia's abdomen. "Your baby must be due about the same time as ours." He looked up. "January, right?"

Alicia nodded, smiling at him.

"Thought so." He paused, and his expression changed to one of desperation. "I want to buy her something pretty to wear for the holidays. We've got several nice parties to go to. You know, glittery business affairs. But she's feeling really unattractive right now and uncertain if she should even go."

Boy, could Alicia relate to that.

"She's not, though." The man's eyes shone with love, and his voice revealed the depths of his feelings. "She's beautiful. Especially now."

Alicia felt a lump forming in her throat. What

would it be like to have someone feel that way about her?

"Janet's about your size and coloring. Can you recommend something?"

She forced another smile, then said, "Come with me. I think I have the dress you're looking for."

Her instincts proved correct. Her customer thought the sequined maternity dress with its long overjacket was perfect, and he left Bundles of Joy a happy man.

But no matter how many others Alicia waited on during the remaining hours of the Father's Sale, she couldn't shake the memory of that man—of Janet's husband—and the way he'd said his pregnant wife was beautiful. There was no denying the longing in her heart to experience a love like that for herself.

By the time she pulled into her driveway at 9:45 that night, Alicia was in a full blue funk. It didn't help that the house was mostly dark. Apparently no one had waited up for her. Rags greeted her by the back door. At least she could count on her trusty dog to be glad to see her. That was something.

In the kitchen Alicia set her purse and car keys on the counter, then checked her answering machine for messages. There were none. She found the mail on the kitchen table. Bills. Three applications for new credit cards. A slew of ads. One magazine. Nothing exciting.

Rosie jumped onto the table, demanding attention with a strident, *"Meow!"*

Alicia lifted her into her arms. "So what did everyone do today while I was working?"

The cat purred.

"You're a regular font of information."

Rosie rubbed the side of her head against Alicia's chest and purred more loudly.

"Whatever it was, it must have worn them out. It isn't even ten o'clock." She set the cat on the floor. "Personally, I'm ready for a hot bath."

She flicked off the light switch and made her way toward her bedroom by the soft glow of several night-lights, strategically placed throughout the house. As she entered the bedroom, she intentionally avoided looking toward the sofa bed. She didn't want to think about Joe right now. Because whenever she thought of him, that longing in her heart grew stronger.

She walked into the bathroom and closed the door, releasing a deep sigh as she did so. She left the over-head light off; here, too, a nightlight was all she needed. She started the bath water, pouring in a capful of her favorite bubble bath. Then she undressed, dropped her clothes into the wicker hamper, and stepped into the tub accompanied by another deep sigh.

It was difficult, at this particular moment, to re-member why going into retail had seemed a good idea back when she'd started her business.

She shut off the water and sank deeper into the tub, a thick layer of bubbles tickling her chin. She closed her eyes and tried to empty her mind. She didn't want to think about the business or her grandfather or the baby.

Or Joe. She definitely didn't want to think about Joe.

The doorknob gave a tiny squeak as it turned. Alicia's eyes flew open as Joe shuffled into the bath-room, clad in a T-shirt and pair of baggy shorts. She realized instantly that he was still half-asleep and completely unaware of her presence.

"Joe!" she called to him in a stage whisper.

He froze in mid-stride.

"I'm in the bathtub."

An uncomfortable moment of silence followed as he turned toward her, his eyes wide open now. She knew he couldn't see anything but bubbles. Still, she felt exposed—and the feeling wasn't all bad.

"Sorry," he said. "The door wasn't locked." Then he backed out of the room.

Her body tingled, as if it had been lovingly caressed. The sensation appalled her. She wasn't about to let her hormones and loneliness completely destroy her common sense. She had to get a grip on her emotions before she did something stupid—like falling hard for Joe Palermo, her holiday husband.

To Joe it seemed an eternity before Alicia came out of the bathroom. And all the time he waited, he kept trying to figure out the right thing to say. He didn't know why it seemed such a big deal. He'd only been after a drink of water, and it wasn't as if he'd seen anything, anyway.

Still, there was something very *married* about being in the bathroom with a naked woman immersed in her bubble bath. Something surprisingly intimate.

The instant the bathroom door opened, Joe sat up. "Sorry," he said again.

"I guess the lock's broken," she answered softly.

"I'll fix it tomorrow."

"Thanks."

He saw her pull back the blankets and crawl into

bed. Again he tried to think of the right thing to say, and again he failed.

Then Rosie hopped onto Alicia's bed and coiled herself into a ball on one of the pillows. A moment later Rags entered the bedroom and laid her ugly head on the mattress close to her mistress's face. A whimper brought the desired response; Alicia stroked the dog's coat.

Maybe it was a good thing she surrounded herself with pets. Otherwise Joe might have been tempted to go to her, to take her in his arms, to kiss her the way he wanted to kiss her. Not those fake shows of affection for her grandfather's benefit, but the kind of kiss a man gave the woman he desired.

That settled it. Tomorrow he was headed for the slopes. Skiing was one of the things that had brought him back to Idaho, and a day at Bogus Basin was sure to take his mind off Alicia Harris. He hoped.

"Alicia."

"Yes?"

"I'll be out of here early in the morning. I'm going up to Bogus to ski."

She was silent a moment, then said, "Okay."

"I'll fill you in on what your grandfather and I did before I go."

"Fine." Her voice was faint, not quite a whisper.

"Good night, Alicia."

"Good night, Joe."

Chapter Seven

Alicia was standing at the stove, frying bacon in a skillet, when Joe entered the kitchen. She saw him hesitate and check the room. Instinctively she knew that if her grandfather had been present Joe would have given her a kiss for a greeting. But since Grandpa Roger wasn't in the room, he stayed where he was.

"I need a screwdriver," he said. "Do you have one?"

"A screwdriver?"

"To fix the bathroom lock."

"Oh." A blush rose in her cheeks. She returned her gaze to the skillet. "In that drawer to your left."

As he opened it, he asked, "By the way, I can't find one of my gloves. Have you seen it anywhere? The black leather ones I use when I'm driving."

"No. Sorry, I haven't."

"Hope I haven't lost it." Screwdriver in hand, he turned and left the kitchen.

Alicia let out a deep breath, at the same time try-ing—unsuccessfully—to rid her memory of last night and the bathtub and Joe.

I'm as bad as I was when I was ten. It's a crush. That's all it is. He's nice and he's good-looking and he's doing me a huge favor. But that's all it is.

It had to be all it was, because this situation was temporary. He'd made it clear he never wanted to marry. Besides, he didn't want children, didn't think he would make a good father.

"I think the bacon's done."

Alicia gasped in surprise. The spatula clattered to the floor as she spun toward the kitchen doorway where Joe stood once again.

"Did you burn yourself?" he asked, striding to-ward her.

"No. No, I—" She clamped her mouth shut with-out finishing her sentence. She couldn't tell him what she'd been thinking.

Joe pulled the skillet off the burner, then scooped the overly crisp bacon onto a paper towel with a fork.

By the time he was finished, Alicia felt a little more composed. "Thanks. You caught me daydreaming."

He glanced over his shoulder. After a moment, he smiled.

There went her pulse again, skyrocketing.

"Have I told you how much I like your pink bunny slippers?" he asked softly. "They're very...*you.*"

She wished her heart would stop fluttering like a captured bird. "That doesn't sound like much of a compliment," she whispered, fighting that infernal blush.

"Well, it is." He touched her cheek with his fingertips.

Her throat was as parched as if she'd walked in the desert for a week straight.

Grandpa Roger's voice intruded on the moment. "Can a third party join you? Or would I be in the way?"

Joe pulled back his hand. "Come on in, sir. Alicia was fixing breakfast."

"Wasn't what it looked like from here," her grandfather said as he entered the kitchen, grinning at them like the Cheshire cat.

"How would you like your eggs, Grandpa?"

"Scrambled is fine."

"Joe? Over medium?"

"No, you can scramble mine, too." He held up the screwdriver. "I need the Phillips. Be right back." He crossed the room, opened the drawer, exchanged one screwdriver for another, then left the kitchen a second time.

"Something broken?" Grandpa Roger asked.

Not yet, Alicia thought. But I'm afraid my heart is about to be.

The ski resort was packed on this first Saturday after Thanksgiving. Snow had come early to these westernmost slopes of the Rockies, and the skiers were out in full force.

While waiting in line at the lift, Joe heard someone say it was the best powder they'd seen in years. He looked forward to getting to the top of the mountain so he could experience it for himself. He needed something to clear his head. He hadn't been thinking like himself. Not since the day he'd met Alicia in that coffee shop.

Darned if he wasn't starting to feel as though they were a family, he and Alicia and her grandfather.

A family. What did he know about being part of a family? An *Ozzie and Harriet* kind of family, that is. Dysfunctional he had no problem understanding.

As the lift swung around and picked him up, he muttered a few choice words beneath his breath. He was feeling too much and working too little. That's all that was wrong with him. Come Monday, he had to make serious changes in his routine. It was up to Alicia to entertain her grandfather during his visit. Let her take some time off work. She was the boss, Christmas season or not. She could jolly well spend time with the old man. Joe wasn't going to do it anymore.

A short while later, he skied off the lift. When he was out of the way of other disembarking skiers, he stopped to adjust his goggles and check his equipment, then he attacked the mountain with a vengeance, hoping to work off the last of his—

The last of his what?

Frustrations?

Irrational expectations?

Attraction to Alicia?

Whatever it was, he wasn't successful. Thoughts of Alicia and her grandfather went down the slopes with him. At the bottom he *whooshed* to a stop, pushed the goggles up onto his forehead and glared back in the direction he'd come, feeling out of sorts with the world.

A child began to wail, drawing his gaze toward the bunny hill. There they were, a group of mogul monsters, taking their ski class. The kid who was crying was probably no more than five years old. Maybe six. While Joe watched, a man strode onto the scene and knelt in the snow in front of the boy. His dad, apparently. The man talked to the kid, dried his tears, smiled reassuringly, and in what seemed no time at all, the boy was back with his class, grinning from ear to ear. The man looked on with obvious parental pride.

Would I make a good dad?

The question nearly knocked him off his skis. There was no way that he wanted to have kids. Not a chance. Never.

He envisioned Alicia, her hands resting lovingly on her enlarged stomach, looking feminine, tender, beautiful.

Oh, no. It just wasn't going to happen. No *way!*

He needed another run at the mountain. Maybe another dozen runs.

"Grandpa, I can't believe how much you've learned in a couple of days." Alicia looked over her grandfather's shoulder at the screen of the laptop computer. "Are you sure you're a novice?"

"It's the gospel truth. I was green as grass until that husband of yours gave me lessons."

That husband of mine…

Grandpa Roger turned his head and glanced up at

her. "I like him, Alicia. I think you found yourself a fine man. I just wish I'd been at the wedding."

"Me, too," she answered softly while returning her gaze to the screen. "What are you looking up now?"

"I actually found a site for retired ministers. Can you believe it?"

"Yes. These days, there seems to be a Web site for everything imaginable."

"Mmm." Her grandfather shook his head, and his voice was grim. "Both good and evil, I'm afraid." He twisted on his chair, then laid a hand on Alicia's stomach. "You protect this little one, my girl. The world is full of traps."

She smiled, but her vision was blurred. "I will, Grandpa. I promise. I'll always take good care of Humphrey."

"Humphrey?" He chuckled as he patted her belly. "I hope you have a better name in mind for my first great-grandchild than Humphrey Palermo."

Palermo? Her heart did another one of those silly little flutters as she pictured Joe holding a tiny baby in his arms.

"So?" Grandpa Roger prompted.

She pulled herself back to the present. "I'm sorry. What were you asking?"

"What names have you chosen for the baby?"

"I'm not…*we're* not sure yet. We've still got time, so there hasn't been any rush to decide."

"No favorites at all?"

She shrugged. "I rather like Alexander for a boy and Jennifer for a girl."

"And what about Joe?"

She couldn't tell her grandfather she'd never asked

her husband's opinion about baby names. So she told another lie: "He can't decide." She shrugged a second time. "You know how some men are. He says he's leaving it up to me to choose."

Her grandfather continued to look at her without saying a word, his gaze thoughtful.

"You know," she said, taking a step backward, "I think I'd better call the shop and see how the day is going."

With that, she turned and beat a hasty retreat to the kitchen where she picked up the telephone handset and held it to her ear.

For months she'd been testing first names with her last name. Alexander Harris or Jennifer Harris. She'd always liked the sound of those two best.

But how would they sound with Palermo?

She pictured Joe again, holding a baby, smiling, crooning softly.

Alexander Palermo…

Jennifer Palermo…

"I've *got* to stop this," she said as she hung up the phone without dialing. "It could never happen. It couldn't happen in a million years."

"What couldn't happen?" she heard Joe ask.

Her heart fluttered as she turned toward the door to the utility room. "I didn't hear you come in," she whispered.

"That's because you were talking to yourself." He smiled, then asked again, "What couldn't happen?"

She shook her head. "Oh, just something from work. Nothing important."

Lying was getting to be a way of life, it seemed.

Lying to her grandfather. Lying to Joe. Lying to herself.

"How was the skiing?"

In his stocking feet, Joe stepped into the kitchen, closing the utility room door behind him. "Beautiful. You should've been there."

She wouldn't have thought it possible, but he appeared even more handsome than usual in his silver-gray ski pants and white turtleneck shirt. His cheeks were ruddy from the cold, and his spiky black hair looked damp. She was sorely tempted to run her fingers through it, try to restore it to order.

Instead she turned her back toward him. "It sounds like you had a good time."

"Yeah. And I plan to go up again soon."

"You should. It's why you moved back to Idaho, after all." Her heart hurt, making it difficult to speak.

"Alicia?"

She heard the soft fall of his stocking feet as he crossed the kitchen.

"Come Monday I've got to spend more time talking to local law firms." He lowered his voice to just above a whisper. "And I should find an apartment, put down a deposit to hold it. I'll need to be ready to move come the first of the year."

She nodded, still without looking at him.

"It'll be here before we know it."

"Time flies," she answered woodenly.

Out of the corner of her eye, she saw him lean his backside against the kitchen counter and cross his arms over his chest. "Where's your grandfather?"

"On the computer." She had to meet his gaze now. "You created a monster."

Joe grinned.

It took her breath away.

She was falling for Joe Palermo. Falling fast and hard.

Big mistake. That's what had happened with Grant. She'd fallen fast and hard for him, and look where it got her. Divorced, pregnant and lying to her grandfather.

Joe watched the confusion swirling in her eyes and wondered what was going on behind them. He wished he could say something that would make her laugh, something that would make her eyes sparkle again.

But he knew better than that. He'd spent the day on the mountain trying to drive her from his thoughts. He'd almost succeeded.

Almost.

He cleared his throat as he stepped away from her, putting some distance between him and temptation. "I think I'll take a shower."

On his way through the living room, he paused long enough to greet Grandpa Roger, then headed for the master bathroom. A short while later he stood beneath a hot spray of water, leaning his forehead against the glass door of the shower stall.

"Temptation?" he whispered, testing the word's meaning.

Yes, temptation.

There was no denying he'd felt flashes of desire for Alicia, and he still found it strange. But there was more to this than physical desire. Much more. It was something warm and tender that seemed to wrap itself around his heart at the mere sight of her, at just the thought of her. Something that made him feel like protecting her from the world, sheltering her from anything that might do her harm.

"I'm losing it," he muttered as he poured shampoo into his hand and lathered his hair.

Joe Palermo had never been and never would be some knight in shining armor riding in to rescue the damsel in distress. Joe was the dragon about to roast said damsel with flames from his nostrils. Like his father before him, he was an aggressive Type A personality, a driven, self-motivated, self-obsessed kind of guy. Men like him made lousy husbands and worse fathers.

Temporary insanity was the only explanation for him being in this house, playing this role, and the sooner he got the heck out of here, the better off he would be. Maybe he should try to convince Alicia to come clean to the old man. In lieu of that, he meant to bury himself in his work until he was rid of all these crazy thoughts.

He turned off the water, then dried his head with a towel before sliding the shower door open.

A half second before he would have stepped onto the rug, he heard a telltale hiss, followed by a throaty feline growl. Rosie was lying in wait near the bathroom door. Her tail flicked back and forth like the bar of a metronome.

Moving slowly, he stepped onto the rug with his right foot. Rosie's growl rose sharply just before she leaped at him. Joe pulled back in the nick of time, sliding the shower door closed. The cat crouched again, tail flicking off the seconds as she waited with infinite patience for her prey to reemerge.

He was trapped. Trapped by an enemy that couldn't

weigh even ten pounds, but trapped all the same. He stood there, in the safety of the enclosed shower stall, pondering his options.

There weren't many. In fact, as far as he could tell, there was only one.

He closed his eyes, clenched his jaw. He breathed in deeply through his nose, then released it through his mouth. Once. Twice. And again.

It wouldn't get him anywhere, putting it off.

"Alicia!" he shouted.

He opened his eyes and looked at Rosie. He would have sworn she was grinning, even while she threatened him with another throaty growl.

"Alicia!"

This had to be the single most humiliating moment of his life.

"Alicia, come here!"

At last there was a knock on the bathroom door. "Joe?" The knob jiggled. "What is it?"

"It's your cat," he answered, trying to control his anger. "She's holding me hostage."

"Rosie?"

He couldn't be sure, but he thought there was a hint of amusement in her voice.

"Yes, Rosie," he snapped. "Get her out of here."

The knob jiggled again. "The door's locked."

"I know it's locked. I fixed it. Remember?"

"Yes…I remember."

He wasn't mistaken. She was fighting laughter. She was almost strangling on it.

"Get…me…out…of…here." He enunciated each word with care.

"Right away."

Joe glared at the ball of orange fur, teeth and claws and swore to himself he would one day have his revenge. He didn't know what it would be, but he would have it. So help him, he would.

Joe's anger was a palpable thing. He still simmered with it as the three of them sat down for supper that evening.

Alicia wasn't making things better by grinning every time she remembered the sight of Joe standing in the shower, a towel wrapped around his waist, his hair damp…and Rosie crouching on the bathroom floor like a lion in wait for a gazelle.

Grandpa Roger cleared his throat. "Pass the potatoes, will you, Joe?"

Joe did so without comment.

"I was telling Alicia about some of the Web sites I discovered today. Fascinating. If you have the time later, I'd like to show you."

Joe grunted something noncommittal.

Alicia and her grandfather exchanged glances. She gave her shoulders a small shrug and did her best not to smile.

Grandpa Roger tried a new tack. "Alicia says the two of you haven't agreed on a name for the baby yet."

Joe's head came up. His gaze shot toward hers.

"Naming your baby is an important decision," her grandfather continued. "The father should definitely participate."

Alicia wasn't feeling quite as amused as she'd been before.

"I remember when Alicia's grandmother was pregnant with Justin. Teresa and I spent hours poring over lists of names. It was a special time for the two of us. Drew us even closer together than we'd been before.''

Alicia looked down at her supper plate. Her appetite had vanished along with her laughter.

"I'd only been home from Europe a couple of months when Teresa discovered she was expecting. After all the destruction and evilness of war I'd witnessed, her pregnancy seemed to be God's reaffirmation of life and goodness. Those months were a joyous time for us both." Grandpa Roger was silent a moment, then added, "But I don't have to tell you two that."

"No, sir."

Alicia kept silent, unable to speak over the lump in her throat.

"'Course, we hoped Alicia's father would be the first of several children, but that wasn't to be. Teresa was never able to carry another baby to term." Grandpa Roger took a few sips of water. As he set the glass on the table, he said, "I hope you'll be blessed with a full quiver."

"Sir?"

"From Psalms. 'Like arrows in the hand of a warrior, so are the children of one's youth. How blessed is the man whose quiver is full of them.'"

Alicia couldn't help herself. Her gaze was irresistibly drawn to Joe. She was surprised to find him looking at her. His expression was inscrutable; she had no idea what he was thinking or feeling.

Her grandfather continued, warming to his subject. "There's a special glow about a woman who's with child. A special beauty. When my wife was expecting, I used to sit in a chair in the living room, right out there, and watch her as she did her sewing or knitting or whatever other busy work she did in the evenings. All I could think was how beautiful she was. Just like Alicia is now.''

She glanced at her grandfather. ''I'm far from beautiful.''

He chuckled softly as he shook his head. ''You're wrong, my dear. Ask your husband if you don't believe me.''

''I feel more like the proverbial bull in a china shop.'' She pushed herself up from her chair. ''Excuse me.'' She left the kitchen in a hurry.

Once she reached the bedroom, she closed the door behind her and sagged against it. Tears stung her eyes. Her throat burned.

Ask your husband if you don't believe me.

''Oh, Grandpa. I wish you were right. I wish Joe thought me beautiful.''

She crossed the room and stood before the full-length mirror. She smoothed her maternity top over her stomach, then turned sideways for a second look.

''Beautiful,'' she muttered. ''Oh, sure.''

The tears returned, and her image blurred.

Chapter Eight

Joe succeeded in keeping himself busy in the days that followed. He was less successful at keeping Alicia out of his thoughts.

On Sunday morning, while she and her grandfather went to church, Joe returned—without apology to the retired minister—to the slopes at Bogus Basin. On Monday, he went to the library, ostensibly to do research, although he caught himself daydreaming all too frequently. And most of those daydreams included Alicia. On Tuesday he not only had interviews with two Boise law firms but he also checked out four apartments in different parts of the city. On Wednesday he spent long hours in the basement of Alicia's home, closing more of his files, preparing to ship them back to his old firm in California.

He spent as little time as possible with Alicia and

Grandpa Roger, pretending it was the demands of work and not because he was avoiding them. He wasn't sure if he fooled the older man or not; he *was* certain he didn't fool Alicia.

He awakened on Thursday morning to the sound of a storm buffeting the old farmhouse. Naked tree limbs whipped the siding and scraped the windows and rooftop. He sat up in bed, listening to the lonely wail of the wind. Rags trotted across the bedroom to beg for attention with a whimper. Joe stroked the dog's head while thinking, *Pest.*

"It's snowing," Alicia said softly.

He glanced in her direction.

She sat up, a shadow in the darkness. "Must be close to ten inches on the ground already."

"Really?"

"Mmm."

He rose on his knees and pushed the curtains aside to stare outside. The back porch light revealed a winter wonderland beyond the window.

"You going in to work today?" he asked.

"Not today."

"Good. The roads will be bad. You shouldn't be driving in this."

They were silent awhile. Rags returned to the side of Alicia's bed, looking for more constant attention than Joe had given her.

"Joe?"

"Yeah?" He sat down again.

"I need to ask a favor."

He waited. When she didn't go on, he said, "What?"

"Grandpa has asked if he can visit my birthing class that starts soon. He wants to go with us."

"Us?"

"Yes." Her reply was nearly inaudible. "Just once, he said."

"Ooh, boy."

"I'm sorry, Joe."

He raked the fingers of both hands through his hair as he said, "I guess it can't be helped. Not unless you decide to tell him the truth. Which wouldn't be such a stupid idea, as I've suggested before."

She hiccuped.

At least, that's what he thought he heard. But a moment or two later he realized she was crying but trying to hide it from him.

He didn't think about the wisdom of his actions. He simply got up and went to her. He sat on the edge of the bed, took her in his arms, held her against him.

"I didn't mean to make you cry," he said when her tears subsided.

Over another choked sob, she answered, "It isn't your fault. It's my own. I got myself into this mess."

"True enough." He smoothed his hand over her hair. "But with all good intentions."

She lifted her face toward him.

He wished he could see her clearly.

She sighed, then said, "I never realized how hard it would be on you."

"I'm a big boy. I can take it." He lowered his head closer to hers.

"Even Lamaze?" she whispered.

"Yes." The word came out on a soft breath.

And then he kissed her.

Alicia momentarily stopped breathing as Joe's mouth covered hers. She stopped thinking, too. All that remained were feelings, sensations too glorious to be defined.

Warm tentacles of pleasure spread through her veins. Warm—yet she shivered. The beat of his heart, so close to her own, gave her a sense of safety, made her feel sheltered. Close—yet she wanted to be closer still. He tasted good. He smelled good.

If he'd asked, she might have given herself to him, right then and there.

He didn't ask.

He lifted his head, then he slipped from her embrace and rose from the bed. She felt alone, bereft, rejected.

"Alicia, I didn't mean to—"

"It doesn't matter," she answered, holding onto her tattered pride for all she was worth. "I understand."

"No, I don't think you do."

He was a man. She was a woman. The woman with whom he was sharing a bedroom. A dark bedroom where he couldn't see how she looked—fat and misshapen. She wasn't going to hold his kisses against him. After all, it was her idea to have the two of them playing married. It would give anyone ideas.

It had certainly given *her* ideas.

She'd assumed that being pregnant had removed all remnants of sexual desire from her system. She'd been mistaken. She wanted Joe with a fierceness she wouldn't have thought possible only three short weeks ago.

Temporary insanity, she told herself. That's all it is.

"I think I'll try to get some work done," he said.

"So early? It's barely five o'clock."

"Yeah...well...I'd better."

He left the bedroom, closing the door softly behind him.

"I disgust him," Alicia told the dog. "He can't get away from me fast enough."

Joe was confused by what he felt. It was something more than desire—although he felt that, too. Man alive, did he feel it! But this was different. This was some strange emotion, wrapping delicate threads around his heart and drawing him into a fantasy he didn't and couldn't believe in. Whatever this was, it was far more dangerous than casual sex could ever be. He knew that on gut instinct alone.

"So get out," he said aloud as he sat at the desk in his temporary basement office. "Tell her the masquerade is over."

But he knew he couldn't do it. He couldn't leave her, couldn't disappoint her. He tried to pretend it was merely his sense of honor that kept him in her home, playing this role. After all, he'd given his word.

Who was he kidding?

That wasn't why he stayed. He stayed because he *wanted* to stay. As simple as that.

Alicia was surprised to find she'd drifted back to sleep. It was the sound of a snow shovel scraping concrete that awakened her the second time.

Feeling groggy and out of sorts, she got up and

walked to the window, slipping into her robe as she went. She pulled back the curtains—and was nearly blinded by the brightness of the snowy morning that awaited her eyes.

Wearing his ski garb, Joe was shoveling the back walk. He worked with a steady, smooth rhythm, sliding the shovel beneath the heavy snow, then effortlessly raising it over his shoulder and letting the snow fly toward the yard.

It's nice to have a man around the house.

She groaned as she turned from the window. How corny could she get? What was she going to do next? Start wearing a shirtwaist dress, heels and pearls while she did the housework? She'd been shoveling her own sidewalks for eleven winters, ever since she inherited this house from her grandparents. She could have shoveled them today, too, even big, fat and pregnant. She wasn't helpless.

Humphrey gave her a stiff jab in the ribs.

"Ouch!" She looked down, touched her stomach. "Well, I could. And exercise would do you good, too, little one."

Scrape...scrape...scrape... The sound drew her gaze back to the window.

"It *is* nice to have his help," she admitted softly.

More than nice...wonderful.

More than wonderful...because it was Joe.

She touched the windowpane with the palm of her hand. "How could I let this happen?" she whispered. "How could I let myself begin to love you?"

She was startled from her discovery by a rap on the door.

"Alicia?" her grandfather said softly from the hallway.

"Yes?"

"May I come in?"

"Yes," she answered, then realized the sofa bed was unmade. She whirled around, wondering if she could reach the door before he—

Too late.

Grandpa Roger smiled at her as he stepped into the room. His smile faded as his gaze fell on the evidence of Joe's sleeping arrangements.

"Morning, Grandpa," Alicia said, trying to sound cheerful and unconcerned.

He looked at her. "Is something wrong, my girl?"

"No." She shook her head. "Why do you ask?"

"You don't usually sleep so late." His gaze flicked to the sofa bed again, then back to her.

She tightened the belt on her robe. "No, we didn't have a fight, if that's what you're wondering." She turned toward the window, hiding from her grandfather's shrewd eyes. "I was very restless in the night. Tossing and turning. Poor Joe had to move to the sofa so he could get some sleep. He's had to do that on a number of occasions lately."

"It wasn't my intention to pry into your marriage."

"You weren't prying, Grandpa. It's okay. I can see how it must look. But things are fine between us. They couldn't be better. You don't have to worry about me. Or Joe."

There was a lengthy silence.

Then her grandfather said, "All right, my dear."

A moment later the bedroom door closed and she was once again alone.

Scrape...scrape...scrape...

"Oh, Joe. If you could—"

But she didn't dare speak her wish aloud. It would only make her heartbreak more complete when January came and Joe was gone from her life for good.

Much as Alicia had been doing when he entered her bedroom a short while before, Roger stood at the window of the guest bedroom and watched Joe shoveling snow off the walk between the back porch and the unattached garage.

Roger Harris hadn't lived to be seventy-seven years old and served fifty-five years in the ministry without learning a thing or two about people. His granddaughter was lying to him; she was as transparent as glass. Things weren't right between her and Joe. It was obvious Alicia loved that young man, and Roger believed her husband returned her love. But sometimes, the way they acted, the way they spoke, it all seemed so...so...

He shook his head, wishing he could put his finger on what was bothering him. More important, he wished he could put his finger on what was bothering them. They were pretending all was well and normal between them.

Deep in thought, he patted his chest with his right hand while pursing his lips. The Good Book said the truth set a person free, and he believed it. The truth was always preferred, even if it was unpleasant.

And if he knew the truth, maybe he could help this young couple find their way.

After two decades in California, Joe had forgotten what hard work shoveling snow was. But it had served a good purpose. He'd worked off a lot of his frustration by the time he was finished.

As he stepped through the back door into the utility room, he smelled breakfast cooking. Waffles and bacon, if he wasn't mistaken.

"Another month here, and my cholesterol's going to be off the charts."

He removed his boots and set them on a rug next to the door. Then he hung his coat on a hook, sticking his gloves in the coat's pockets. He hesitated before taking his first step toward the kitchen door. He wanted to make certain Rosie wasn't lying in wait for him.

Man, how he hated that cat.

The coast appeared clear, so he proceeded toward the kitchen, wondering what he should say to Alicia, if he should apologize again for kissing her.

But it wasn't Alicia whom Joe discovered standing at the counter, removing a golden-brown waffle from the waffle iron. It was Grandpa Roger.

"Hungry?" the older man asked without looking over his shoulder at Joe. "I figured you must've worked up quite an appetite, clearing all the walks."

"I could eat." He glanced toward the living room. "Where's Alicia?"

"In the shower, I think. I heard the water running a while ago."

Joe considered again whether or not he should tell Alicia he regretted what had happened earlier, try apologizing better a second time. Only he didn't regret kissing her. Not really. He only regretted the complications that came with the interest he was feeling in her. If circumstances were different—if she wasn't carrying another man's baby, if she weren't the type of woman who wanted husband, home, family—he would have welcomed a relationship with her. She was pretty and sexy and interesting.

When she isn't crying, that is.

As if reading his mind, Grandpa Roger said, "Pregnant women aren't always easy to live with."

"What?" Joe looked at Alicia's grandfather.

"I said, pregnant women aren't always easy to live with." He carried a platter of waffles and bacon to the kitchen table.

"Is *any* woman?"

Grandpa Roger chuckled. "You have a point." He motioned for Joe to sit down. "Alicia said she wasn't hungry yet, so we'll go ahead without her."

After Joe sat down, the older man blessed the food, then passed the platter across the table.

"The bacon is all yours." He sighed, a sound of true regret. Then he continued, "When my wife was expecting Justin, I never knew what would upset her. Seemed I was always making an egregious error of one kind or another. If she wasn't crying, then she wasn't speaking to me."

Joe nodded. "Alicia's the same."

"And during those last months of her pregnancy, I hardly got a single good night's sleep. My, how Teresa tossed and turned. Sometimes she even talked in her sleep. Alicia ever do that?"

"Not that I've heard," he answered. "But then, I'm a sound sleeper. I can sleep through almost anything."

Grandpa Roger looked thoughtful as he said, "Lucky you."

Joe had the strange feeling he'd said something wrong, although what it could be, he hadn't a clue.

The older man filled his juice glass, then took a few sips. Afterward, he set the glass on the table, his right index finger tapping the rim as he softly said, "Love covers a multitude of sins."

"Sir?"

"Oh, I was simply reflecting on how forgiving Teresa was of all my human frailties. Without that ability to forgive, our marriage never would have lasted fifty-three years."

"Fifty-three years?" Joe let out a soft whistle. "That's a long time."

Grandpa Roger smiled. "Yes. And worth every bit of effort to make it last, too." He took another sip of juice, then asked, "What about your parents? How long have they been married?"

"They divorced while I was in law school. Mom's remarried now. Dad's come close a few times to taking another plunge, but he hasn't ever gone through with it. I don't think he ever will. He's soured on marriage." He almost added, Like father, like son.

"That's a shame."

Joe shrugged. "I guess so. But my folks were miserable when they were together, so I guess the divorce was better for everybody all the way around."

Rags trotted into the kitchen, nails clicking on the linoleum, interrupting whatever the older man might have said next. Right behind the dog came Alicia, her hair still damp from the shower. She wore a hot-pink maternity top with big black polka dots on it. Beneath her blouse, she had on a pair of black leggings. On her feet she wore those silly bunny slippers of hers.

She looked adorable.

Made Joe wish he could kiss her again.

"Good morning," she said as she stopped behind her grandfather's chair. "Thanks for making breakfast." She kissed him on the top of his head. Then her eyes shifted to Joe. "You had a busy morning."

"Yeah."

"The walks look great."

"Had to be done. Gotta be able to get to the cars."

She went to her chair and sat down.

"Are you ready for a waffle?" Grandpa Roger asked as he lifted the platter.

"No. Just juice, thanks."

Joe passed her the carton. "Are you feeling all right?"

"I'm fine." She didn't look at him.

"Don't forget you're supposed to be eating for two," he said, surprising himself.

It seemed to surprise her, too. She glanced up; their gazes collided.

After a moment he smiled at her. A few seconds more and he realized it was important that she smile at him in return. More important than it should have been *if* he hoped to avoid further emotional entanglements.

Which he did.

Didn't he?

Chapter Nine

The following Saturday was another hectic day at Bundles of Joy. Only three weeks before Christmas, the shopping madness was in full swing.

Alicia had hired several seasonal sales clerks, but there still didn't seem to be enough help. There never seemed to be a moment for anybody to sit down and rest their aching feet, let alone for Alicia to take her customary catnap.

It was nearly four o'clock when she finished ringing up the customer she'd been helping, a woman who was outfitting the entire nursery for her son and his wife, who were expecting a baby in the spring.

"It's the least I can do for my first grandchild, don't you think?" the woman had said. "I'd nearly given up on them ever having children."

As the woman left the store, Alicia noticed Joe

standing near the shop doorway, watching her. She had no idea how long he'd been there. She glanced around, looking for her grandfather, but he was nowhere to be seen. Immediately, she felt a spark of alarm.

"Where's Grandpa?" she asked as she hurried toward Joe.

"I left him napping in front of the TV."

"Is he feeling all right? He isn't—?"

"He's fine. You need to quit worrying."

"I just thought…when I saw you alone—"

"Can't a man come to take his wife out to dinner, if he wants?"

Her heart skipped a beat.

"Even if she's a make-believe wife?" he finished with a conspiratorial wink.

Disappointment flooded through her. For just a moment she'd thought, she'd hoped—

"Your grandfather considered it a good idea."

"Be honest. It was his idea to start with. *He* put you up to this, didn't he?"

Joe gave her a wry smile. "He's a hard man to argue with. I'm learning I might as well just go with the flow."

She nodded in agreement. "I won't be finished here until six."

"That's okay. I don't mind waiting. I'll do some Christmas shopping and come back for you."

Who would he be shopping for? Alicia wondered.

As if she'd spoken the question aloud, he said, "What is it you want for Christmas?"

"Me? But you don't have to buy me a—"

"Yes, I do. What would your grandfather think if

I didn't give you a gift for our first Christmas to-gether?''

She sighed. ''I guess you're right. I suppose you'd better tell me what you want to find under the tree, too. A wife should know these things.''

''Surprise me.'' His grin broadened, and his gaze seemed to caress her cheek. ''I love surprises.''

''Do you?'' she asked, feeling breathless again.

He leaned closer, lowered his voice. ''Yes, as a matter of fact, I do. Don't you?''

''I'm not sure,'' she answered in an equally soft voice.

She'd been surprised by her feelings for Joe Palermo; she loved him more than she'd thought possible. But had she *liked* that surprise? No, not when she suspected how much it was going to hurt later on.

She took a step back from him. ''I'd better see to my customers.'' She turned. ''I'll see you at six.''

Downtown Boise was aglow with Christmas lights. Store windows were draped with garlands of green, the glass sprayed with frosty-white images of elves and bells and pine trees, the displays enticing. The chilly December wind hadn't kept shoppers at home. Even this late in the afternoon, the sidewalks and department stores and small specialty shops were filled with men, women and children in search of the perfect gifts for their loved ones.

Stopped outside a dress shop, Joe turned up his coat collar and stared at a pretty party dress of aquamarine chiffon in the center of the window display. The color matched Alicia's eyes. It would look great on her—in a couple more months.

He shook his head. He didn't want to give her something she couldn't use now.

He turned and continued down the sidewalk.

Alicia hadn't told him what he should get her for Christmas. Not even a clue. She wouldn't need anything for the baby. She could buy those things wholesale. Besides, he wanted his gift to be just for her. Something personal. Something for Alicia alone.

What did a man buy for a wife who was still a stranger to him?

He stopped at the corner and waited for the light to change, giving him permission to cross the street. A squeal of joy caused him to turn and look behind him. A couple—no more than twenty years old, either of them—stood in front of a jewelry store display, kissing each other with abandon, mindless of all the staring passersby.

Young love. At first it seemed his thoughts mocked them, but after a moment he realized it was envy he felt, not disdain.

The light changed and the crowd surged around him, but Joe didn't move. He watched the couple go into the jewelry store, their adoring gazes still locked upon the other. He couldn't seem to help himself. He followed them.

Inside the store, he observed the couple as they leaned over a display case filled with wedding and engagement rings.

"Pick the one you like best," the young man said to his fiancée.

"No, I want the one *you* like best," she answered.

They kissed again, their eyes open, as if they couldn't get enough of the sight of one another.

A sales clerk arrived at Joe's side. "May I help you find something, sir?"

"No, I—" He stopped himself abruptly, changing his answer. "Yes. I'd like something special...for my wife." He glanced at the clerk's name tag. Bridget, it read.

"Do you have anything in mind?" Bridget asked.

"I'm afraid not." He shrugged. "I'm not very good at this sort of thing."

"Approximately how much did you want to spend?"

He shook his head, then shrugged again.

"Why don't you step this way? We have a nice selection of earrings. Does your wife have pierced ears?"

He had to think for a moment before he could answer, "Yes."

"Perhaps she would like some diamond earrings." She smiled at him. "I've never known a woman who could have too many diamonds."

That statement would have fit his ex-wife, he thought as he followed Bridget, and it would have fit many of the women he'd dated over the years since his divorce.

But Alicia?

He imagined her in that oversize pink bathrobe and wearing those silly bunny slippers. He grinned. For some reason, diamonds just didn't fit the picture.

"Not diamonds," he said to himself as he veered away from Bridget.

He found what he hadn't even known he was seeking in the display case farthest from the store's entrance. A ring with two small pearls and a cut stone the same blue-green as the dress he'd seen earlier. The same blue-green as Alicia's eyes. The ring was dainty, understated. Perfect for Alicia Harris.

"Did you find something?" Bridget asked when she caught up to him.

"There." He placed his index finger on the glass. "That ring there."

"Oh, that's a lovely choice. Let me get it out for you." She leaned down to unlock the back of the case. "What size ring does your wife wear?"

"Size?" *Darn!* "I'm afraid I don't know for sure. Her hands seem small to me."

Bridget raised her eyebrows, and Joe suspected it took great effort for her not to roll her eyes, too.

"Let me see your hand," he said. When she did, he continued, "Looks to me like about the same size. Try it on."

She placed it on the third finger of her right hand. It fit perfectly.

"I'll take it," Joe said with a smile, already imagining Alicia's look of surprise when she opened her gift on Christmas morning.

Alicia's back was killing her and so were her feet. "Sit down and rest," Susie ordered in a motherly tone. "I'm perfectly capable of closing the till without your help."

Alicia decided not to argue; she sank onto a nearby stool that was tucked behind the counter.

Her assistant manager glared at her. "You need to take time off until after the baby comes."

"I'm fine. The doctor doesn't think I need to stop work until—"

"I don't care what *he* thinks. Look at you. You're exhausted."

"But this is our most important time of the year."

Susie straightened, tilting her chin upward in defiance. "Are you saying I can't be trusted to manage the store properly, Ms. Harris?"

"Of course not." Alicia released a deep sigh.

"Then stay home and enjoy your grandfather. He came all the way from Arizona to be with you, and his health isn't the best. You don't know how many more opportunities you'll have to be with him."

"That's true."

A rap on the locked door drew both of their gazes. There was Joe, motioning to be let in.

"Stay home and enjoy *him*," Susie added.

Without comment, Alicia pushed up from the stool and walked—actually, it was more of a waddle—toward the entrance. She turned the dead bolt, then pulled the glass door toward her, allowing him in, along with a blast of frigid air.

"It's really turned cold," Joe said as he faced her. "You ready to go?"

Alicia glanced at Susie. "I'm ready." She wouldn't have dared say anything else. "I'll get my coat."

"No," he said. "Stay here. I'll get it for you. You look beat."

His comment made her feel fat and frumpy, completely unattractive. She knew he hadn't meant it that way, but that was the effect, nonetheless. Maybe it would be better if they went straight home and forgot going out to eat. It was her grandfather's idea, anyway, not Joe's. He wouldn't mind. He would probably be glad if she changed their plans.

When Joe returned, Susie said to him, "You make sure she eats a good supper. She needs nourishment, and she's been working way too hard."

"I'll make sure," he answered.

"I told Alicia she ought to go on maternity leave now, but she won't hear of it. See if you can talk some sense into her."

Joe looked at Alicia, one eyebrow slightly raised. "I'll try."

She sighed.

"Ready?" he asked, holding up her coat.

"I'm ready." She turned around and slipped into the sleeves.

"Then let's go. I'm starved." He took hold of her arm, then glanced over his shoulder. "'Night, Susie."

"Good night, you two. I'll lock the door behind you. Have a good time."

Joe's grip on Alicia's arm tightened as they stepped outside into the wind. "My car's in the parking garage across the street," he said as he steered her toward the crosswalk. "I thought we'd go to Malloy's. Is that okay?"

"Fine with me."

It wasn't far from downtown to the restaurant on Broadway Avenue, but heavy traffic caused it to seem farther. It was a good thirty minutes before they pulled into the parking lot at Malloy's Seafood Bar and Grill. They had to park in back.

"Looks as if we might have a wait," Joe said when he opened the passenger door for her.

"As long as there's a place to sit down."

He took her arm again. She liked the feel of it. Maybe this wasn't such a bad idea...even if she did "look beat" as Joe had so indelicately put it earlier.

He, on the other hand, looked as marvelous as ever. Alicia was aware of all the women in the restaurant who stopped what they were doing or saying in order to stare at him.

Hands off, ladies, she thought. He's mine.

But he wasn't hers. Not really. And the futility of her situation cut through her like a knife through the heart.

"We're in luck," Joe said after speaking to the maître d'. "They can seat us now. Come on."

Their table was in a small alcove, giving the illusion of private dining. Alicia was grateful for that. She needed some isolation from crowds and noise.

Joe helped her off with her coat, then pulled out the chair for her. She mumbled her thanks as she sat down.

The waiter handed them each a menu while telling them that evening's specials. "I'll be back in a while to take your order," he said before hurrying away.

Joe smiled at Alicia. "Remember what Susie said. You need nourishment."

What I need is you, Joe. More than I should. More than is wise. I never meant for it to happen, but it did.

After a few failed attempts to jump-start a conversation, Joe decided to allow Alicia to eat her supper in peace. Not that she did much of a job of it. It seemed to him that she spent more time moving food around on her plate than actually consuming it.

He was about to ask what was troubling her when,

all of a sudden, she whispered, "*Oh!*" Then she smiled tenderly, her hands touching her sides.

Joe's gaze followed hers to her abdomen, and he was amazed to see her maternity top move, as if driven by a wave beneath the surface. "What was that?"

"The baby."

It happened again.

"The baby?" he echoed inanely.

She looked at him, still smiling. "I get tired, and Humphrey gets active. Happens all the time."

"I've never seen it before."

She was silent a moment, then asked, "Would you like to touch? Feel it for yourself?"

"I don't know…"

"It's okay if you do. I don't mind."

"Are you sure?" He was surprised to discover he *did* want to feel it.

She took hold of his hand, placing it on her belly. "I'm sure."

He waited…and waited…and waited. He was about to give up when something moved beneath his hand. Something strong and almost sharp.

He looked up, meeting her gaze. "What *is* that?"

"Most likely a knee or an elbow. Could be a heel."

"And this happens often?"

She laughed. "Often enough."

"Does it hurt?"

"No. Not usually, anyway."

He drew back his hand. "Amazing."

Joe would have had a difficult time finding the words to express himself better than that. He'd never paid much attention to the idiosyncrasies of pregnancy. He'd certainly never before placed his hand on an expectant woman's stomach and felt a baby move. He'd known a few men who'd gone overboard in their enthusiasm for future fatherhood, and he'd secretly made fun of them. What was the big deal, after all? Women had been carrying babies and giving birth to them since time began, and they'd be doing so long after Joe Palermo had breathed his last.

But now he thought he understood, at least a little, what those men had felt.

He wasn't sure he liked knowing.

"Joe?"

"Yeah?"

"Grandpa thinks we...he thinks you and I...he thinks we're having trouble in our marriage."

"What gave him that idea?"

"He came into the bedroom the other morning and saw the unmade sofa bed." She looked down at her abdomen again. "And he's probably noticed other signs as well."

"Signs?"

Her gaze flicked to meet his, then turned toward the window. "I thought it would be easier than it is. To pretend we're married."

"We've been doing a pretty good job, all things considered."

"But we don't act like two people in love," she replied softly, still staring out the window.

He remembered the young couple in the jewelry store, the way they'd gazed into the other's eyes with complete adoration. Had a woman ever looked at him in that same way?

"I know it isn't easy," she added. "I'm not very attractive these days."

"You're wrong."

That caused her to look his way again.

"You're wrong," he repeated. "You are attractive."

"You don't have to be kind, Joe. I wasn't fishing for compliments."

"And I'm not serving them up, either."

The air grew thick and still. He thought about kissing her. Kissing her and much more.

Joe would never know what might have happened next. The appearance of their waiter with the check broke the spell that had fallen over them.

A short while later they left the restaurant. Neither spoke during the long drive home.

Chapter Ten

Joe didn't sleep well that night. He heard every creak the house made, every breath Alicia took, every whimper from Rags, even Rosie as she padded down the hall on one of her nocturnal inspections. That would have all been bad enough if he'd understood *why* he couldn't sleep, if he could have pinpointed the reason and then dealt with it. But it wasn't that simple. This had more to do with fuzzy impressions and disturbing, unnamed emotions than with anything concrete.

Joe always dealt better with the concrete than with the abstract.

He had just checked the clock for the umpteenth time—7:00 a.m.—when Alicia let out a sharp gasp. It was unmistakably a sound of pain.

"Alicia?" He sat up. "What's wrong?"

"Nothing." The word was barely out of her mouth when she caught her breath again.

He got up and hurried across the room. Leaning close, he ignored Rosie's warning growl. "What is it?"

"Just a stitch in my side. That's all."

He took hold of Alicia's hand. "Are you sure?"

"I'm sure." She pulled her hand away, then sat up, leaning her back against the headboard.

Joe didn't move.

"Stop hovering," she snapped, obviously irritated. "I'm all right."

"You didn't sound all right a minute ago."

"Well, I am."

He straightened but remained at the side of her bed. "I think Susie's right. You need to stop working until after the baby comes."

"Don't be ridiculous."

His sudden anger was irrational, and he knew it. But that didn't change it. At least he managed to keep from raising his voice. "*I'm* not the one being ridiculous. I'm telling you, you need to stay home."

"And who do you think you are to tell me what to do? My *husband?*"

"No, I don't think I'm your husband." Joe switched on the bedside lamp so he could see her. "But I *do* think I'm the one with the common sense."

Alicia crossed her arms over her chest. Her eyes sparked with an anger that matched his own. "My work schedule is *none* of your business." She enunciated each word with care.

"It is as long as we're playing this little charade of yours," he replied with the same precision. "Your grandfather would expect it. Remember? Even a guy like me knows you need to rest and take better care of yourself. At least think about the welfare of the baby.''

Her face paled. "How dare you?'' she whispered.

"I dare plenty when I care enough.''

Alicia pressed her lips together in a thin line. Her chin quivered.

Joe couldn't be sure if she was stifling a colorful retort or fighting tears. Maybe both. He decided he'd better get out before he said something he would really regret. He'd probably already said more than he should have.

"You're single and over twenty-one,'' he said as he turned away. "Do what you darn well please.'' He grabbed his sweats and slippers off the chair beside the sofa bed, then strode from the room.

Before he reached the stairs to the basement, his outrage had evaporated. Alicia was right. It wasn't any of his business. She could decide what was best for herself.

But darn it all! He *did* care about her. He cared plenty.

He cared too much.

From his basement office Joe heard the water running in the master bathroom.

I've gotta apologize to her, he thought. *I was way out of line.*

He booted up his laptop, listening as it whirred and clicked, making all its usual odd sounds before it was ready for his first command. He considered opening his word processing program and doing a bit of work, but he logged on to the Internet instead, hoping a visit to one of his favorite sites would take his mind off of Alicia.

He looked over the snow reports for Bogus Basin, Brundage Mountain, and Sun Valley. He priced new skis, boots and poles. He even checked on a two-week vacation package to a resort in Switzerland.

Alicia remained all the while in his thoughts.

He wasn't sure what possessed him to go to a search engine and enter the word "maternity" in the search box. The first links in the list of Web sites didn't improve his spirits: complications of birth; difficult births; breech delivery.

Then he found some options on birthing classes. Curious, he followed the links and began reading.

By the time he heard footsteps on the stairs outside his cramped office, he had a passing knowledge about the Lamaze and Bradley natural childbirth methods, understood about birthing rooms and "mother-friendly" hospitals, and had printed off a copy of Ten Tips for a Healthy Pregnancy as well as several pages of frequently asked questions.

He closed his Internet browser just as Grandpa Roger appeared in the doorway.

"Am I intruding?" the older man asked.

"No. Not at all. I was about ready to go upstairs and get myself something to eat."

"Mind waiting a minute or two?"

Joe shook his head. "No, sir."

Alicia's grandfather settled onto a wooden chair that had seen better days; it rocked slightly on its uneven legs. The elderly man's expression was grim. Apprehension tightened Joe's belly.

"You know," Grandpa Roger began after a pregnant pause, "I've rather come to like you in the short while I've been here."

"Thank you, sir. The feeling's mutual." He had a bad feeling about this.

"You and Alicia seem right for each other."

Uh-oh.

Grandpa Roger's eyes narrowed as he looked across the desk at Joe. "Society's mores have changed a great deal during my lifetime. Not always for the better. In some circles nowadays, marriage is considered passé." He gave his head a slow shake. "I'm not part of those circles, Joe. I remain firmly convinced that men and women should wed before they are physically intimate, and I most definitely believe they should be legally joined in matrimony before they bring children into the world." He leaned forward. "Do you think those beliefs are antiquated, young man?"

"Ah...no, sir."

"Good. Then will you tell me why you haven't married my granddaughter?"

Joe glanced toward the stairway, then back at the older man.

"I overheard your argument this morning," Grandpa Roger continued. "I put two and two together and got four. You've arranged some elaborate hoax for my benefit."

"Sir, I—"

"Do you love her?"

What else could he say? "Yes. Yes, of course I do."

"And you want to participate in raising your child, give him a good home?"

Again, he had no choice but to answer "Yes."

"Then I expect you to do right by them both. I expect you and Alicia to get married. If you love her and want to be a part of her life and your baby's life, then there's no reason you shouldn't."

"Mr. Harris...sir...well, you see, the reason we haven't—"

"Good Lord!" The dread on the older man's face might have been comical if it hadn't made him look as if he were about to suffer another heart attack. "You're not a married man, are you?" He clutched his chest with both hands. "You don't already *have* a wife?"

"No, sir, I'm not married. I was once, ten years ago. I never planned to go through that again."

Grandpa Roger visibly relaxed. "I see. Once burned, twice shy. Is that it?"

Joe nodded. It was true, after all.

"Children?"

"No. The marriage was brief. Six months."

"Ah."

Joe rose from his chair. He would have paced the office, only there wasn't enough room. "I think I should talk to Alicia."

"That was my thought, too."

"I'll go now."

Grandpa Roger stood. "We'll go together."

"But, sir, I—"

"You'll find I'm a stubborn old man, Joe, when I choose to be. This is one of the times I choose to be."

* * *

Alicia stared at her reflection in the mirror over the sink. There were dark circles under her eyes, and her complexion was pallid.

Maybe Joe and Susie were right.

She winced inwardly, hating to admit that, even if only to herself.

"I *am* tired," she said to her reflection. "Terribly tired."

She hoped her grandfather would understand when she told him she wasn't going to church this morning. She didn't have the energy.

She sighed, realizing she owed Joe an apology. He'd been concerned for her welfare. Maybe he'd overstepped his bounds a little, but their argument was entirely her fault. She'd been out of sorts and had made him pay for it.

She turned from the sink and left the bathroom. No point putting it off. She would make her apologies now.

Joe and her grandfather were standing in the middle of the living room when Alicia emerged from the hallway. Something in Joe's expression caused her to stop in her tracks.

"We need to talk," Grandpa Roger said.

Joe gave an almost imperceptible shake of his head, followed by an equally subtle shrug.

"Let's all sit down," her grandfather added. "Shall we?"

Apprehensive, Alicia sat in the wing chair closest to the piano. Joe sat across the room from her in the recliner. Grandpa Roger settled onto the couch.

Does he know? she wondered as she met her grand-

father's gaze. She quickly looked at Joe. Did you tell
him?

As if he'd heard her silent question, Joe gave another slight shake of his head.

"Alicia, my dear girl, I overheard your argument
this morning," her grandfather began.

Her heart sank as her worst fears were confirmed.
She lowered her gaze to a spot on the hardwood floor,
about three feet in front of her.

"I can only surmise why you have concocted this
pretense. I suspect it was to protect me. For my
health."

She nodded.

"I won't judge you, Alicia, for the choices you've
made. It isn't my place to sit in judgment. But I'd be
in error if I didn't encourage you to do what your
heart knows is right. I've witnessed the love you and
Joe have for each other. Your baby should have the
privilege of seeing it, too."

"Oh, Grandpa," she whispered, her misery clear
in those two words.

He continued, his voice gentle but firm. "Whatever
impediment you perceived that kept you from marrying before now, it can be overcome. And I hope, if
the impediment was my reaction when you called me
last spring, that you can forgive me for my careless
words."

She looked up, knowing the moment had come to
tell the truth. The whole truth. "Grandpa, I think you
should know that—"

"Your grandfather's right," Joe interrupted, rising
to his feet. "We should get married." He stepped
toward her, skirting the coffee table. "I told him

about my being divorced and never intending to marry again. But he's right. That's no excuse. We should do as he says.''

"But, Joe, we can't—"

He knelt beside her chair. "We can work things through, Alicia. I know we can." He took hold of her hands, pressing them together between his. His eyes beseeched her not to argue with him. "Marry me."

She could scarcely think over the din of her pounding heart.

"Say yes."

In some remote part of her brain, she knew this couldn't really be happening, that she was dreaming, and any moment now she would wake up.

"Say yes," Joe repeated, his voice low and beguiling.

"Yes," she whispered, staring deeply into his beautiful brown eyes.

Her grandfather stood. "You two should be alone."

She was aware of Grandpa Roger leaving the living room, heard the click of his bedroom door closing behind him, but her gaze never strayed from Joe. Not even for an instant. She wanted the fantasy to continue a little longer. She wanted to believe in the love her grandfather thought he saw. She wanted to pretend she was carrying Joe Palermo's baby and that he loved her and wanted to marry her, wanted them to be a family.

Joe shattered the romantic daydream with a few softly spoken words.

"Good thing you played along." He released her hands, then rose to his feet. "I think the shock might've killed him. You should've seen him down in the basement. I was really worried.''

She blinked.

''I'll draft a prenup agreement that'll protect us both,'' he continued, just above a whisper. ''The marriage can be dissolved after your grandfather goes back to Arizona.''

Her throat ached, and her chest hurt.

Joe leaned down, touched the back of her hand, forcing her to look at him once again. ''It'll be okay. It's only for a few weeks. I can be convincing in my role as the new husband. I've come to care for your grandfather too much to let anything happen to him because of me.''

''Thanks, Joe,'' she managed to say.

His smile was tolerant. ''Don't look so sad. We'll pull this off. Your grandpa's gonna be okay.''

''Sure he will.''

The real question was, would *she* be okay?

Chapter Eleven

Joe was as good as his word. His prenuptial agreement, which he presented to Alicia on Tuesday morning before she went to work, covered all the bases.

"I had another lawyer look it over," he assured her. "He's got plenty of expertise in domestic law. We don't want any unforeseen problems later on. It was his idea to add this clause."

He pointed to a section of the document.

The clause specified that Alicia's baby was not Joe's offspring, and he would not now nor at any future time be expected to provide financial support for it.

The daddy clause, she thought sadly as she read it a second time.

Or, to be more accurate, the *non*daddy clause.

Suppressing a sigh, she signed the document and

handed it back to Joe without comment. She would rather die than let him see how wounded she felt by it all. She was doing this for the sake of her grandfather, she kept telling herself. For her grandfather and no other reason.

But even for Grandpa Roger she wouldn't change her mind about where to have the wedding. They would be married by a judge at the county courthouse. Period. No argument. Her grandfather would be one witness, Susie Notter would be the other. No invitations. No announcements. No celebrations. Nice and simple.

"I'm eight months pregnant," was the only explanation she would give her grandfather for her decision. "I don't want a church wedding and all the fuss that goes with it. It would be rather inappropriate at this juncture, don't you think?"

Only to herself did she admit the real reason for her choice of civil ceremony—because she couldn't bring herself to speak false vows before a man of the cloth. She couldn't pledge before a minister to remain with Joe "until death do you part" when the truth was they would part in a matter of a few weeks. This was what her favorite novels called a marriage of convenience. It wasn't meant to be real and lasting.

On Friday morning, five days after her grandfather had confronted them in her living room, Alicia, Joe and Grandpa Roger got into Joe's SUV and drove to Boise. It was snowing again, and it took twice as long as normal to reach the city-county building in west Boise. Susie was waiting for them by the main doors.

"Judge Smith's in court now," a woman behind the counter told them while checking her wristwatch.

"But he can marry you during his next break. About another half hour, I'd guess." She motioned to an empty wooden bench. "Have a seat, and I'll call you when he's free."

"Thank you, miss," Grandpa Roger said.

Joe cupped Alicia's elbow with his hand and guided her to the bench. "Can I get you anything while we wait?" he asked.

She shook her head, reminding herself that he was just playing his part—the solicitous bridegroom.

"Well, I'm thirsty," he said as he glanced down the corridor, first to the left, then to the right. "I'll be over at the water fountain." He pointed.

"I'm going with him," her grandfather said.

"It wouldn't hurt you to smile a little," Susie whispered in her ear after the two women sat down beside one another. "It's your wedding day."

Smile? Alicia couldn't remember how. "What am I *doing* here?"

"What you need to do." Susie took hold of her hand and gave it a comforting squeeze.

Alicia looked toward the water fountain.

Grandpa Roger *seemed* well enough. She'd seen no signs of ill health this week, no indications his heart was acting up. He walked more slowly than he used to; he slept later in the mornings and took a few naps during the day. But didn't most people his age slow down and sleep more? Joe had said Grandpa Roger had looked ghastly on Sunday morning when the two of them talked alone. That being the case, she *must* be doing the right thing, for her grandfather looked wonderful this morning.

"What I need to do," she said, repeating Susie's words like a mantra.

"There aren't many guys who would agree to this. Joe must care about you a lot."

"He's very kind."

As if realizing the two women were talking about him, Joe turned his head and met Alicia's gaze. He smiled, then winked at her.

She forgot to breathe.

"Ow!" Susie protested. "Let up."

Alicia looked at her friend.

"You're breaking my hand."

She glanced down. "I'm sorry." She released her grip. "I didn't—" She stopped abruptly, not knowing what she'd intended to say. She lifted her gaze, tears welling in her eyes, blurring her vision. "Oh, Susie."

"Ohmigosh! You *love* him!"

Alicia shook her head in denial, at the same time closing her eyes.

"Yes, you do."

This time she nodded.

"Look at me," Susie commanded.

Reluctantly Alicia obeyed.

"Does Joe know how you feel?"

"No."

"You should tell him, Alicia."

"I can't."

"But—"

"He doesn't want marriage, Susie, and he doesn't ever want kids. I want both of those things. I want them a lot. Joe and I don't have a future together, so it wouldn't serve any purpose for him to know how I feel."

Susie shook her head slowly.

"I'll get over it," Alicia added in a barely audible voice.

"Will you?"

"I'll have to." She released a sigh. "What choice do I have?"

Joe hadn't imagined he would ever again repeat wedding vows to anyone. But there he was, standing before Judge Smith in the judge's chambers—papers, file folders and books cluttering desk and floor— promising to be a husband to Alicia Harris. He knew it was in name only and temporary besides, but he felt as though it was real, all the same.

What surprised him was that it felt real...and he didn't seem to mind.

In fact, he felt amazingly lighthearted.

Maybe that had something to do with the woman at his side. She looked lovely in her ivory-colored maternity dress with its long sleeves and delicate lace collar. He couldn't imagine any bride looking prettier. Still, he wondered if she minded not having all the usual bride's trappings—white gown of satin, lace and pearls, a bridal veil, a church full of flowers and friends. She deserved all of those things.

"Do you have rings to exchange?" the judge asked, interrupting Joe's thoughts.

"Yes."

Alicia glanced up, clearly surprised by his answer.

He removed the ring—the one he'd planned to give her for Christmas—from his pocket. "I hope it fits," he said softly.

She watched as he slipped it onto the third finger of her left hand. Then she looked at him again.

"It matches your eyes," he added, feeling an explanation of some sort was necessary.

"It's beautiful. But I didn't get a ring for you."

He answered her with a smile, only vaguely aware that the judge was continuing with the ceremony.

In less than two minutes more, the judge pronounced them husband and wife. Joe gave Alicia a kiss, keeping it brief and dignified. Afterward, all parties signed the license as required by law, Joe paid the judge his fee, and it was over.

Beaming with joy, Grandpa Roger hugged Alicia, then Joe. "I'm so pleased.... This is wonderful.... God bless you both...."

When Susie embraced Joe, she whispered, "You take good care of her. You hear me?"

"I hear you." He was bemused by the pointed look she gave him when she stepped back. It was as if she were trying to tell him something more, but he had no idea what it might be.

"I'm taking us all out to eat," Grandpa Roger announced. "My treat."

"That isn't necessary, Grandpa."

Joe took hold of Alicia's arm. "Yes, it is." He leaned in close to her ear. "He wants to do it. Let's let him."

She replied with a nod, but he sensed her continued reluctance.

The four of them—Grandpa Roger, Susie and the newlyweds—left the judge's chambers and walked toward the main entrance of the courthouse.

"You'll come to eat with us, won't you, Miss Notter?" Grandpa Roger asked.

"Can't. Gotta get to the shop. My boss is a really tough cookie." Susie grinned as she glanced over her shoulder at Alicia. "Right?"

"Right," Alicia replied with a smile of her own.

But Joe noticed the smile never reached her eyes, and that bothered him. He wanted her to be happy today.

He wanted her to be as happy as he was.

The truth hit him like a pro boxer's punch to the solar plexus. He nearly stumbled over his own feet in his surprise.

Happy? To be married?

Okay, so he knew it was temporary. That could explain it. Their marriage was as much pretend now as it had been before a few words were spoken and a piece of paper signed.

Still...Joe Palermo, happy to be married?

Impossible!

Alicia was miserable.

What had she done to deserve this? Married twice in one year and neither of them destined to last more than a few weeks. Was she so unlovable?

It was ridiculous to think such things, she argued with herself. This had nothing to do with whether or not a man could love her.

But neither of your husbands *did* love you, she thought.

And she shouldn't compare the two men or the two marriages, anyway. Grant had used her, but Joe had done her a favor. Joe cared enough about both her

and her grandfather to carry on this pretense for
Grandpa's sake. He was kind and generous and
thoughtful and…and she loved him.

Which brought her back to *why* she was miserable.

Seated next to Joe in the half-empty restaurant, Alicia cast a furtive glance in his direction.

My husband.

Something warm and torturously sweet coiled in
her belly. At the same time, pain pierced her heart.

Oh, Humphrey. I wish Joe was going to be your
daddy.

Tears blinded her.

"Excuse me," she whispered as she slid from the
booth. "I'm going to the rest room." She hurried
away before either man could see that she was about
to cry.

In the ladies' room, Alicia leaned her back against
the locked door and let the tears fall. She'd been holding it in all week, but now she let her pent-up hurt
and frustration and loneliness and fear and anger
come sobbing out. She cried because she was married
and still alone. She cried because she wanted what
she couldn't have. She cried because she'd believed
in happily ever after, and that belief had been stripped
from her.

When the storm had finally passed, she stepped
over to the sink and stared at her reflection in the
mirror. Her eyes were bloodshot, her eyelids puffy,
her nose red. Black streaks of mascara ran down her
cheeks.

"The beautiful bride," she whispered as she turned
on the water and moistened a paper towel.

When she'd married Grant, she'd been blissfully,

ignorantly happy. Infatuated by his charisma. In love with being in love. She hadn't known she'd married a jerk who would be cheating on her before the ink on the license was dry. Grant had never been kind to her. Not like Joe.

She met her gaze in the mirror again.

Not kind like Joe...

She looked down at the ring on her hand, at the blue-green stone and pearls. It was truly a beautiful ring, a costly one if she knew anything about jewelry. But it was the gesture behind the ring that meant the most to her.

It hadn't occurred to her to buy a ring for him. Not knowing, as she did, the way he felt. A ring would have proclaimed to the world that he was a married man, and that was something he didn't want to be.

It matches your eyes.

The memory of his words, of the way he'd looked at her as he slipped the ring on her finger, caused a fluttering sensation in her stomach.

Would a man who felt nothing for his bride have noticed that the stone was the same color as her eyes? Wasn't there a chance—even just a glimmer of a chance—that Joe had acted out of more than mere kindness? Wasn't there a chance it wasn't only concern for her grandfather that had caused him to marry her instead of letting her tell the truth?

Hope came surging back. Perhaps without reason. Perhaps without wisdom. But there it was—hope.

"I've got three weeks," she told her reflection. "Three weeks before Grandpa leaves. I'm not going to waste them feeling sorry for myself."

* * *

Joe was beginning to worry. Alicia had been in the ladies' room a long time. Maybe he should check on her. She'd looked kind of pale when she'd left the table. Maybe she was sick. Or maybe she'd passed out. Women did that sometimes when they were pregnant; he'd read that the other day when he was on the Internet. Maybe she was lying unconscious on the bathroom floor.

Those thoughts had no more passed than he saw Alicia coming through the restaurant. Relief spread through him. Their gazes met as she drew near. She smiled, and for the first time today, her smile appeared genuine.

"You okay?" he asked.

"I'm fine." She slid into the booth beside him. "Sorry I took so long." Her gaze remained locked with his.

She had the most amazing eyes, Joe thought. Like the crystal blue-green ocean found in warm climes such as Hawaii or the Caribbean, like those beaches and coves where people went snorkeling. He had the absurd feeling that if he could dive into her eyes, like a snorkeler into the ocean, he would find beautiful surprises beneath the surface, surprises more precious than pearls and coral and bright-colored fish.

Embarrassed by his own imagination, Joe felt heat rising up his neck. He'd never been given to romantic notions like those. He'd never understood poetry that compared a woman to a summer's day. He was the practical sort, logical and levelheaded in all circumstances. Or at least, he used to be. He hadn't acted like himself for weeks.

"Have you ordered?" she asked.

"We were waiting for you." He was thankful he sounded halfway normal.

"I'm suddenly starved." She looked at her grandfather. "I guess my case of nerves is finally over."

Funny. Joe was just beginning to feel nervous.

"Drop me off at the Senior Center on your way home," Grandpa Roger said as Joe drove his vehicle out of the restaurant parking lot an hour later. "You two should have this day to yourselves."

Alicia liked the idea.

"Are you sure, sir? There's not likely to be many people at the center with these roads as slick as they are. We didn't have anything special planned for this afternoon."

Apparently Joe didn't feel the same way.

"I'm sure," her grandfather answered. "You don't need an old man hanging around the house." He tapped Joe on the shoulder. "You should get yourself a suite at the hotel. You could take your bride out to supper, go dancing, hold her through the night in a bed with a fancy canopy."

"*Grandpa!*"

"Even brides who are eight months pregnant want some sort of honeymoon, my girl."

She looked down at her round belly. She didn't know if lovemaking was even permissible, healthwise, at this stage of her pregnancy, let alone if she would *want* to participate. But she *did* know she'd like to lie in Joe's arms for a night, to sleep with her head on his shoulder, to breathe in the scent of him as she ran her fingers over his bare chest.

She felt suddenly warm and leaned forward to turn down the car heater.

Grandpa Roger tapped Joe on the shoulder again. "You drop me off at the Senior Center. I'll find my-self a ride home later."

"Sir, I really don't—"

"Don't argue with your new grandfather, my boy."

Alicia turned her gaze out the passenger window. Snow continued to fall in huge wet flakes, blanketing everything in white.

Pristine, clean, fresh, new. If only she could have come to Joe as such a bride. Not that she would wish away Humphrey. She wanted her baby. She already loved him. Or her. But still she couldn't help wish-ing...

She felt Joe's hand close over hers where it rested on the center console. Despite herself, she looked his way.

"Your grandfather's right," he said softly. "Every bride deserves some sort of honeymoon. What would you like to do?"

I'd like you to hold me and kiss me and tell me you love me.

"Alicia?"

"Let's just go home, Joe."

"Okay." He glanced over his shoulder, then back at the road. "We'll plan a honeymoon for after the baby arrives, Grandpa Roger."

Oh, how she hoped that would turn out to be true.

They left Alicia's grandfather at the Senior Center as he'd requested. The rest of the drive was made in silence. Once at the house, Joe parked the SUV as close to the back door as he could get. Then he hur-ried around to the passenger door and helped Alicia to the ground. He took a firm hold of her arm with his left hand while he slipped his right arm around her back.

He'd done the same thing a number of times in the past few weeks, but for some reason, he felt more concerned for her safety now. He didn't want her falling and hurting either herself or the baby.

Was this the way all husbands felt toward their expectant wives?

They reached the back porch door without mishap. Joe opened it, then let Alicia go in ahead of him. He caught up with her before she reached the door into the utility room.

Even if Joe had been grilled for hours by the finest attorney in the country, he couldn't have found an answer for what happened next. He was as surprised as Alicia when he swept her feet off the floor and, cradling her in his arms, carried her into the kitchen.

"Joe, what are you doing?"

"I'm carrying my bride across the threshold. That's what."

"Well, put me down. I'm too heavy."

"You're not too heavy," he said softly, even as he obeyed her command.

She didn't move away as he'd expected. Instead, she tipped her head and looked up at him, her gaze filled with a woman's unfathomable secrets.

He was the one to take a step backward. "I suppose it was a crazy thing to do."

"Joe..." She reached out, touched his chest with the tip of her fingers. "I...I want you to know how much I appreciate your friendship. You've done so much for me and Grandpa."

He wondered if her gratitude was what he really wanted.

"But you don't have to pretend our marriage is real when Grandpa isn't around. I don't expect you to. Let's just continue to be friends. Let's not allow this charade to get in the way of that."

"I suppose you're right," he replied, recognizing the wisdom of her words.

So why did he feel disappointed?

Chapter Twelve

Alone in the house for the first time in five days, Joe stood in the center of the nursery, his left arm resting on the top step of the ladder. Spread around him on the floor were a bucket, several double-roll bolts of prepasted wallpaper, a can of paste, two brushes, a sponge, a wall scraper, a razor knife, a straightedge and two rollers. On the table next to him were a pencil, tape measure, chalk line, level and pair of scissors. In his hand he held a booklet the clerk at the paint and wall-covering store had told him to read before he got started.

He grinned, thinking how surprised Alicia would be when she got home. Just yesterday she'd told her grandfather that she'd meant to paper the nursery months ago but never got around to it. Now, she'd said, it would have to wait until after the baby came because she was simply too big and awkward to do the work. Her comment had been followed by a deep sigh that had said volumes more than her words.

Joe didn't want her to have to wait. The nursery should be just what she wanted now, not later. It seemed to him Alicia had to put off too many things. He'd like to see her happy. Really and truly happy.

His grin faded, replaced by a frown.

Something had changed between them in the days since their wedding. Except nothing had changed. Which made no sense at all. That sort of dichotomy didn't sit well with him. He wanted things to make sense, including his feelings for Alicia.

But maybe they *did* make sense. Maybe he just needed to admit them, at least to himself. He cared about her more than he'd expected to. She'd somehow become an important part of his life.

He looked forward to seeing her each morning in her pink robe and slippers, her short hair disheveled. She invariably wore a soft smile, no matter how early the hour.

How did she *do* that?

He looked forward to listening as she and her grandfather talked about her girlhood. He liked hearing her laughter, a sound that invaded the darkest corners of his heart. There were times when he looked at her—times when she placed her hands on her round stomach and tipped her head slightly to the side and smiled that secret smile, looking as if someone had whispered something wonderful in her ear—that he thought her the most beautiful woman in the world.

He gave his head a slight shake. This wasn't the time to analyze his feelings for Alicia.

"You think too much, Palermo. Just get to work."

Besides, what did it matter what he felt? In less than three weeks her grandfather would be gone, Joe would move into a place of his own, and their lives would go in different directions, Alicia's consumed by the demands a baby made on its mother and Joe's returning to the normal demands of his profession. That was as it should be.

He glanced at the booklet in his hand, then tossed it aside unread. How hard could it be to hang wall-paper? He'd asked the clerk plenty of questions while picking up the supplies. He didn't need this, too.

He grabbed the level and pencil off the table. Both Alicia and her grandfather had said they would be home between four and four-thirty. That didn't give him much time to finish his surprise.

Alicia was reaching for a stuffed toy on a top shelf when a sharp pain shot through her. With a gasp she doubled over, cradling her abdomen with her arms.

"Alicia!" Susie's hand alighted on her back. "What is it?"

She drew a few slow breaths before she attempted to straighten.

"Alicia?"

She shook her head. "Nothing," she finally managed to answer. "Just one of those twinges I get every now and then."

Susie looked at the customer who was obviously uneasy about the situation. "Let me get someone else to assist you." She called to Judy to help the woman find what she wanted, then she took hold of Alicia's arm and said, "Come with me."

Alicia was propelled by Susie's firm grasp toward the back room. Once there, with the door closed behind them, Susie made Alicia sit down. Then she stood guard over her with arms crossed in front of her chest.

"I'm all right, Susie. You can leave me to rest a moment. I won't need long."

"No."

"Really. I—"

"Alicia, you're putting on your coat, and I'm taking you home, and you aren't coming back until your baby is at least six weeks old."

"Susie—"

"I mean it. If you don't cooperate, I'll tell your grandfather the truth about your divorce from your baby's father *and* I'll tell Joe you're in love with him."

Alicia stared at her friend, silenced by the threats.

"You think I won't do it," Susie continued, "but you're dead wrong. I *will* do it if you don't do exactly what I'm telling you now. I know Bundles of Joy's procedures as well as you do. I can balance the tills and manage the checkbook, and I'm better at hiring and firing than you ever were—except when you hired me, of course." She punctuated her last comment with a saucy grin.

"But it's almost Christmas." Alicia wasn't ready to admit defeat.

"So?"

"So we're shorthanded as it is."

Susie's expression turned serious again. "The store is having its best Christmas season ever. You can afford to hire a couple more people. And I'll work every day if I have to. It isn't worth the risk for you to stay.''

It was Susie's last words that made up Alicia's mind for her. There was no way she could continue to argue when faced with the possibility of risk to her baby. Besides, she *was* tired, and those sharp, unexpected pains *did* alarm her.

''You win,'' she said softly.

''About time.''

''But I can get home without you chauffeuring me.''

''Are you sure? The roads are still slick in spots.''

Alicia nodded, then pushed herself up from the chair. ''I'm sure. I drove myself to work. I can drive myself home.''

''Well...okay. But you call me when you get there.''

''I will.'' Impulsively, she gave her friend a hug. ''Thanks, Susie.''

''No prob. You just take care of yourself. And make sure that husband of yours does his part.''

She turned toward the coat rack. ''Joe's always helpful.'' She suppressed a sigh. ''You can rest easy. I'm in good hands.''

Joe had measured and cut, according to the advice the clerk had given him, but he hadn't taken into consideration that he would need to match the pattern, too.

Obviously hanging wallpaper was a little more difficult than he'd anticipated.

He looked at the pile of wet, soggy, discarded paper. He'd pulled a strip off the wall just moments before. If he kept this up, he would run out of paper before the room was finished. Not a good thing, according to the clerk at the paint store. He seemed to recall there was a problem with matching lot numbers or some such thing.

Maybe he should look at those instructions, see what else he might be doing wrong. A glance at his watch told him he didn't have time to *find* the booklet, let alone read up on the fine art of hanging wallcovering. He needed to hurry if he was going to finish before Alicia got home.

He laid the new strip of paper on the table, then moistened the backside with the paint roller before slapping on some wallpaper paste with a brush. As he carried the paper to the stepladder, he noticed the drops of paste on the hardwood floor.

"I hope this stuff cleans up okay," he muttered.

Getting up the ladder while keeping control of the sticky wallpaper wasn't exactly easy, but he made it without too much trouble. His skills seemed to be improving by small increments.

It would've helped matters if this old farm house had walls that were truly plumb. Matching both the paper pattern and getting a straight alignment were not easy tasks. And the paste didn't seem to want to adhere the way he thought it should.

Again he wondered about that instruction booklet.

He muttered a few choice words beneath his breath as he tried to smooth wrinkles out of the paper, working his way slowly from ceiling to floor. He had just knelt on the floor and was reaching for the utility knife when something cold fell on his head and back.

"What the heck!"

Then he realized the paper had come off the wall and had landed on him in one big, gooey mess. He pushed it off, but the paste remained in his hair, on his clothes, smeared across his arms and even one side of his face.

That's how Alicia found him.

She couldn't help herself. She burst out laughing.

Joe stopped trying to wipe off the paste with his fingers and swiveled toward the door. The expression of mixed surprise and disgust on his face only made his predicament seem all the more amusing.

"It's not *that* funny," he said as he got to his feet.

Alicia nodded, covering her mouth with her hand, trying to hide her smile. "Yes, it is."

"Only because it didn't fall on you."

A renewed fit of giggles kept her from replying.

"I was trying to do you a favor." He kicked away the paper that was stuck to his shoe, then took a step toward her. "Have you no appreciation?"

He wasn't really angry, was he?

But even that threat wasn't enough to stifle her laughter. If he could only see himself, he would laugh, too.

"I warned you."

Before she could react, he was across the room. He grabbed her with his paste-covered arms and pulled her close. Then he kissed her.

If what he'd meant to do was silence her laughter, his methods worked.

Alicia's mind went utterly blank. There was only the feel of his arms, only the taste of his mouth, only that uniquely masculine scent that was Joe's alone. Almost of their own volition, her arms snaked around his neck. Her lips parted slightly, allowing his tongue to spar with hers. She wondered if he could hear or feel the riotous pounding of her heart.

I love you, Joe. I love you. I love you. I love you.

He cradled her face between the palms of his hands before drawing back slightly. Their gazes met and held.

"What're you doing home so early?" he asked, his voice almost gruff.

"I'm officially on maternity leave." She forced a smile. "Susie wasn't taking no for an answer."

"Good for her. It's what I said ten days ago. Remember?"

She wished he would kiss her again. She hungered for his kisses. Instead, he removed his hands from her face and took a step back. She had no choice but to let him move out of·her arms.

"I'm sorry I laughed," she said, forcing herself not to step forward, not to seek his nearness again.

He shrugged, and a wry grin curved the corners of his mouth. "I must have looked pretty funny, at that."

She smiled, though she didn't feel like it now. "Yes, you did."

"I thought it'd be easy." He grabbed a sponge from the work table, then reached out and wiped paste from one of her cheeks. "Sorry. Didn't mean to share the mess."

"It'll wash off."

He turned his back to her, looking toward the partially papered wall. "I wanted to have it done before you got home."

"It was sweet of you. Really. I mean it."

"It needed to get done." He glanced over his shoulder, a twinkle in his eyes, his brows raised. "I should've read the instructions."

"I love you, Joe." She hadn't planned to tell him, but she shouldn't have been surprised when she did. The feelings—her love, her joy, her hopes, her dreams—had become too big to hold in any longer.

Her joy was short-lived.

The look on his face said it all.

A heavy silence filled the room; it pressed upon her chest, threatening to crush her, body and spirit. She would have given anything to be able to unsay the words.

He turned fully toward her. "Alicia..."

"No." She stopped him with a raised hand. "Don't. Let's pretend I didn't say that." She faked a laugh. "Can we blame it on my pregnant-hormones? I blame them for everything else."

He continued as if she hadn't spoken. "You know I care for you, Alicia, and I'm sure you care for me. We're good friends, like you've said before. But it isn't love. It can't be. And even if it was, I'm not good husband material."

Here came those blasted tears. She blinked, trying valiantly to keep them from falling.

"Alicia, I—"

She laid her fingertips against his lips. "I know. You're right. We're too different. We want different things." She pulled back her hand. "It would be the height of stupidity to believe we could make a marriage work."

"Well, maybe not *that* bad."

She knew he was trying to lighten the mood with his teasing.

It didn't work.

"Maybe you should leave," she whispered. "Maybe it's time to tell Grandpa the truth about us and put an end to this sham."

Logically, Joe knew she was right. It was time for him to go, for them to stop playing house. It was time to tell the truth.

Yet, everything inside him rebelled against it.

They stood there, in the middle of the nursery, amidst the disarray of his disastrous wallpapering attempts, their gazes locked. He could see his own confused emotions mirrored in her eyes, and he wished he could wipe it away for both their sakes. If he could find the right words...

But before he could try, the sound of the back door slamming shut intruded.

Alicia turned away from him. "That'll be Grandpa." She left the nursery, her back straight, her head held high.

She's going to tell him now.

Alarm shot through Joe, and he immediately followed her as she headed for the kitchen. He didn't know what he intended to do or say. He only knew he wanted to stop whatever was about to happen.

But what happened wasn't what he'd expected.

"Grandpa!" Alicia cried.

Joe stopped in the kitchen doorway, taking in the scene before him. Grandpa Roger had collapsed on one of the vinyl chairs. His arms hung loose at his sides while his head rested on the table surface. His eyes were closed. He looked unconscious.

"Grandpa?" Alicia touched his shoulder.

He groaned in response.

"Joe, call for an ambulance."

He was already headed for the phone.

"Wait." Her grandfather sat up slowly. "I don't need an ambulance." His words were whispery thin.

Joe held the receiver in his hand; he could hear the drone of the dial tone. "Are you sure?"

"I'm sure. Just help me to my room. I only need a short rest."

"But Grandpa…" Alicia began.

Her grandfather took hold of her hand. "Relax, my girl. It's not a heart attack. I'm overtired. That's all."

Alicia glanced toward Joe, her eyes filled with fear.

Joe figured it wasn't wise to argue with him. Better to do as he said and call the doctor later.

He placed the receiver in its cradle, then crossed to the table. "Ready?" he asked as he put one arm around the elderly man's back.

"I'm ready."

"Okay. Here we go." With care, he helped Alicia's grandfather stand. "We'll go only as fast as you want, sir. You set the pace."

Grandpa Roger nodded. "Sounds good." He glanced over his shoulder. "Would you get me a glass of water, my dear? I'll want to take one of my pills."

"Right away." Her voice quavered.

"Do what you can to comfort her," Grandpa Roger said softly as he and Joe left the room. "I don't want her making herself sick over me."

"You worry about yourself. I'll take care of Alicia."

"I know you will, Joe. And it does my heart good to see the way you love her. Does my heart good."

By the time Grandpa Roger was lying on his bed, covered with a handmade quilt, Joe had to admit he didn't look too sick. His coloring was good, and he seemed to be breathing normally. He hoped Alicia was coming to the same conclusion as she hovered near the bedside, watching as her grandfather dutifully swallowed his pill.

"I'll leave the door open, Grandpa," she told him. "You call if you need me."

"A nap is all I need, and I'll be fine." He waved his hand in a gesture of dismissal. "Now go on, both of you, and let me be."

Alicia obeyed with obvious reluctance.

As they stepped into the hallway, Joe thought she looked in far worse shape than her grandfather. From the telltale quiver of her chin, she was fighting tears.

"He's going to be fine," Joe promised as he drew her into his arms. "You'll see."

Alicia hid her face against his chest. "Oh, Joe, I was so scared."

"Your grandfather's okay." He kissed the top of her head. "We'll take him in to see the doctor if it'll make you feel better." He patted her back. "Don't worry, Alicia. Don't worry. He's going to be fine."

Roger Harris rolled onto his side, turning his back toward the bedroom doorway. He didn't want to take any chance of one of them seeing his self-satisfied grin.

Maybe he should have gone onto the stage. He seemed to have a natural flair for the theatrical. And he'd set the plan into action in a matter of moments. If either Alicia or Joe had heard his earlier arrival, it never would have worked.

He pursed his lips as his conscience niggled him. Lying was a sin, of course. Any minister knew that. But this wasn't *completely* a lie. He *was* tired. He *could* have collapsed with fatigue. And hearing Alicia say it was time to end her marriage *had* caused his chest to hurt.

No, he didn't regret his little pretense. As long as it kept those two together long enough to work through their differences, then he trusted the good Lord would forgive him.

I love you...

In the wee hours before dawn, Joe stared up at the ceiling and let the memory of Alicia's words play over and over again in his head.

I love you, Joe.

Was it possible she really loved him? That she wasn't merely grateful for his help? And if it was love she felt, what did she want from him in return?

He suppressed a groan.

He might not know the answers to the first two questions, but he knew the answer to that last one. She would want marriage. She'd want the real thing.

He'd been inches from a clean getaway, he told himself. She'd told him to leave, that they were going to end the charade once and for all. If not for her grandfather's weak spell that afternoon, Joe would've been out of there. Gone. Vanished from her life.

Wasn't that what he wanted?

He wasn't the type for a committed relationship.

His first marriage had proven that. He liked his work too much. And what free time he had, he preferred to spend pursuing his own interests. He was too selfish to think of someone else before himself. He was like his old man in that regard.

And he sure as heck didn't want to be thinking about kids! He'd watched his friends and business associates go through the rug-rat years, not to mention the even worse teen years. Those people were never able to simply take a vacation whenever and wherever they liked the way Joe could. They were always in need of baby-sitters before they could go out for dinner or to a movie. They were always running off to doctor or dentist appointments or meetings with the principal. Their lives were run by the needs of their kids.

Who wanted that? Not *him!*

Alicia mumbled something in her sleep.

The reason he'd stayed was because she'd needed a favor from him. But that was the only reason he stayed.

Wasn't it?

He sat up in the darkness.

What if he was wrong about his reason? What if all the things he'd thought about marriage—and about himself—were in error?

I love you, Joe.

He looked toward Alicia's bed. The nightlight had burned out, and he couldn't see her. He was tempted to rise and cross the room, to stare down at her while she slept.

He resisted the temptation, but there was no denying the desire he felt to hold her close, to taste her sweet kisses, to hear her joyous laughter, to see her gentle smile. There was no denying that the past month had changed him somehow. It had been days—weeks really—since he'd given a serious thought to finding a new firm and practicing law again. He hadn't even returned to Bogus for another day on the slopes.

Why not?

I love you, Joe.

He lay down, closed his eyes, tried to make his mind go blank, to quiet the churning questions. But there was one that wouldn't be ignored.

If he had a chance for something more in his life, if he had a chance to really love and be loved, would he take it or would he let it slip away?

Chapter Thirteen

Pale morning light fell through the nursery windows. Long icicles, hanging from the eaves beyond the glass, cast odd shadows across the hardwood floor, a floor covered with ruined wallpaper. It was rather emblematic of the mess she'd made of her life, she thought as she stuffed another strip into a large garbage bag.

She heard water running in the shower and knew Joe was up. She released a deep sigh. They needed to talk about what had happened yesterday, but she wasn't sure she was ready yet.

Holding the garbage bag over her shoulder, she left the nursery. She paused at the guest room door and peeked inside. Her grandfather still slept. She was thankful for that. She meant to make certain he spent the day right there, except for a visit to the doctor.

She continued her way to the kitchen where she pressed the button on the coffee maker to start it brewing. Then she carried the garbage bag through the utility room and deposited it on the back porch. Rags had completed her morning inspection of the yard by this time and dashed into the house while the door was open, obviously glad to be out of the sub-freezing weather. Alicia paused long enough to ruffle the dog's ears before filling both food and water dishes. Those chores finished, she reentered the kitchen.

Joe was waiting for her there.

"You didn't have to clean up the nursery," he said as she closed the door behind her. "I would've done it."

She shrugged. "I didn't mind. I was awake."

He paused, then asked, "How's your grandfather this morning?"

"He's sleeping peacefully. But I'm going to ask him to see the doctor."

"Probably a good idea. It would make *you* feel better if nothing else."

"You're right about that."

He looked out the window.

She glanced down at Rags, standing next to her, tail wagging.

"Alicia—" he began.

"Joe—" she said at the same time, looking up again.

They both stopped, their gazes locked.

Finally he said, "You first."

"About yesterday."

"It's okay. You don't have to explain."

"You're wrong, Joe. I *do* need to explain. Or at least talk about it. We can't pretend it didn't happen."

For a moment she thought he might disagree.

But then he nodded and said, "Let me get my coffee first."

She breathed a silent sigh of relief as she sat at the table.

I wish I didn't love you, Joe. It would make everything so much easier.

Coffee mug in hand, he sat opposite her. He looked entirely too handsome, too self-confident, too much like an attorney.

She lowered her gaze to her hands, clasped atop the table. "When I suggested you help me by pretending to be my husband, I never imagined things would get so complicated."

"I know that."

She gave her head a quick shake but didn't look up. "Don't interrupt, please. Let me get it all said."

"Okay."

"I was ready to tell Grandpa the truth. You know I was. But after yesterday's spell, I'm back to being afraid what the truth would do to him." Her hands clenched more tightly. "I can't take the risk. Not as long as I have a choice."

"I'm not asking you to risk it. I plan to see this through."

"I know you will." Now she looked up. "Because that's the sort of man you are."

He frowned a little, as if not sure what she meant.

"Joe, I'm not going to ask for more than you can give. I shouldn't have said I loved you." Silently, she added, *I do love you, but I shouldn't have said it.*

He opened his mouth, then closed it without speaking.

She gave him a small smile of thanks. "What I'm asking is that we go back to behaving like friends again. We like each other. There's even some mutual attraction, I think." She had to look away, suddenly afraid he would deny even that much. "After all," she continued, her voice soft and quavery, "we're a man and a woman living in close quarters. I suppose a few kisses were inevitable. It's natural."

Above the rapid beating of her heart, she heard the tick of the clock on the wall and the soft *whir* of the refrigerator.

Shoring up her courage, she lifted her gaze to meet his. "It would make it so much easier during the next fifteen days if we remembered we were friends first. Then it won't be so hard to pretend we're anything more." She extended her hand toward him. "Fair enough? Friends?"

The clock continued ticking; the refrigerator kept on whirring.

"Fair enough," he said at last, taking hold of her proffered hand. "Friends."

She wondered how it was possible for her to smile while her heart was breaking.

That evening Joe took hold of Alicia's arm and helped her out of the vehicle.

"Are you nervous?" he asked as they walked toward the medical clinic's entrance.

"I don't think so."

"Good thing one of us isn't," he joked.

She laughed, a pretty sound in the crystal cold night.

Joe was glad for it. He was glad for the talk they'd had, glad they'd cleared the air. He was glad she'd realized she wasn't in love with him, that they were good friends and nothing more.

Inside at the front desk, Alicia asked for directions to the birthing class.

"Right through that door and to your left. In the conference room. You can't miss it."

The woman was right. They couldn't miss it. Four other couples had arrived before them. The women were all well along in their pregnancies. One looked as if she must be carrying triplets, triplets who could make their entrance at any moment.

Joe didn't feel much like joking now.

An attractive woman in her thirties—the only one not obviously pregnant—approached Alicia and Joe with an outstretched hand and a welcoming smile. "Hello. You must be the Palermos." She shook Alicia's hand first, then Joe's. "I'm Pat Grisham, your instructor. We were just about to get started with a video." She motioned toward a grouping of chairs in front of a television set and, speaking to everyone in the room, said, "Please take your seats."

If anybody had told Joe two months before that he would find himself surrounded by pregnant women while watching a video of a live birth, he'd have told them they were insane. But there he sat. And the odd thing about it was, he found it fascinating. Okay, the video made him a little squeamish, but it was still fascinating.

He wondered what it would be like to be present in the delivery room, watching as his child was born.

When the tape ended, Pat Grisham turned off the television and faced the five couples. "So...are we ready for delivery?"

Nervous laughter swept through the group.

"I guess you know it's too late to back out now," the instructor said.

It wasn't too late for him, of course. He wasn't going to be around for the delivery of Alicia's baby. He wasn't the father.

He looked at the other couples, husbands and wives awaiting new additions to their families. One couple was incredibly young, no more than late teens or early twenties. Another couple looked to be in their forties. The other pairs were somewhere in between, more like Joe and Alicia.

Like Joe and Alicia.

Like a husband and wife.

Like a couple.

The Palermos.

Strange. That didn't sound as bad as he might have expected.

For the most part, Alicia had been happier today. She was determined to simply love Joe and take pleasure in what they had now, this moment, and not to worry about tomorrow.

But when Ms. Grisham instructed each husband to reach around his wife and place his hands on her abdomen, Alicia was reminded how much she'd ached for his touch. Now that she had her wish, she wanted it to *mean* something, too. To *really* mean something.

"Humphrey's active tonight," Joe said softly near her ear.

The warmth of his breath on her skin caused gooseflesh to rise along one arm.

"It's an amazing thing, isn't it?" he continued.

"Awesome." She knew he was talking about the baby, but her heart was talking about something—or rather, someone—else.

"Dads," their instructor droned on, "don't be surprised if your wives say some rather...shall we say, *unkind* things to you during her labor."

Despite herself, Alicia leaned the back of her head against Joe's shoulder and closed her eyes. It was incredibly easy to pretend he was truly her husband, that he was the father of her baby. It was easy to imagine going home with him tonight and crawling into bed and snuggling close. It was easy to imagine his mouth covering hers, his hands stroking her body, his touch gentle, yet stirring.

"Hey," Joe whispered, "what are you smiling about?"

"Nothing much." Without opening her eyes, she rolled her head from side to side. "Just thinking."

"Must be happy thoughts."

"Very," she whispered. "Very happy thoughts."

"How was your class?" Grandpa Roger asked them upon their return home.

Joe helped Alicia out of her coat. "It was fine," he answered.

"We watched a video of a baby being born." There was a teasing twinkle in her pretty eyes as she looked at him. "Joe turned green around the gills."

"I *what?*" he protested in mock indignation.

Her smile brightened. "It's true, and you know it." She turned to her grandfather, who was seated at the kitchen table, and gave him a kiss on the cheek. "I thought Joe was going to pass out, Grandpa. It was sad. Very sad."

"She's telling a whopper, sir. Don't believe a word of it." Joe leaned against the counter and crossed his arms over his chest. "The instructor warned the men about irrational behavior and unkind remarks. I see she was right."

Alicia laughed. "She meant *during* labor."

"Does that mean you're just practicing being irrational and unkind?"

"I have not yet begun to fight." She punctuated the famous quote with a flourish of an invisible sword.

"Wish I'd felt up to visiting your class," Grandpa Roger said as he rose from his chair. "But if there's going to be fainting and fighting, it's just as well I stayed home." He gave Alicia a return kiss on the cheek, then smiled warmly at Joe. "A word to the wise, my boy. Accept the fact that the wife, especially when pregnant, is always right. It will make things much easier on you."

"Thanks, sir. I'll take your advice under consideration."

"Good night, you two."

"Good night," they answered in unison.

Once her grandfather had left the kitchen, Joe returned his gaze to Alicia. "Would you like a cup of tea?"

"That would be nice." She covered a yawn with the flat of her hand.

"Tired?"

She nodded.

"Why don't you get comfortable while I fix it for you?"

"Sounds wonderful. Thanks, Joe."

Alicia returned to the kitchen five minutes later, wearing her sweats and slippers. Rosie followed her mistress into the room. The cat stopped when she saw Joe near the stove, then she arched her back and hissed, announcing her displeasure.

Joe wondered if a hot teakettle, thrown from six feet away, could kill a cat. "Maybe I should find out," he said to himself.

"Find out what?"

He kept staring at Rosie. Only the cat's tail twitched; otherwise, she was motionless.

"Joe?"

Suddenly Rosie darted out of the room, as if she'd guessed what he was contemplating.

Triumphant, Joe grinned. "It wasn't anything important."

"Hmm." Alicia sounded suspicious.

The kettle's whistle rescued him from having to say more, and he was thankful for that. He didn't want to spoil the evening by saying *again*—that he hated her cat.

He filled a mug with hot water, then carried it and the variety box of herbal teas to the table. "Here you go."

"Thanks."

He sat down across from her and watched as she

selected her tea bag, dropped it into the cup, stirred until the color was right.

"You were a good sport tonight," she said softly.

"Good sport?"

She glanced up. "You know what I mean."

"Hey, I enjoyed myself."

An arched eyebrow proclaimed her skepticism.

"It's true," he protested—and meant it, much to his continuing surprise.

She smiled, then sipped her tea.

He wondered why it bothered him so much that she didn't believe him. He couldn't even say he blamed her. He'd made it clear he wasn't interested in kids and all the things that went with them.

And yet he hadn't minded a single minute of the class. Not even the video. He wasn't sure how to describe his feelings, except to say he'd felt a part of something important.

"Joe?" Alicia set her mug on the table. "Would you help me get a tree tomorrow? We need to make things more festive around here. For Grandpa's sake if for no other."

"Sure. Be glad to. There was an article in today's paper about a place to chop down your own tree."

He was about to tell her what else the article had said—about the horse-and-sleigh rides, the barbecued ribs and hot chocolate, and the carolers—but she spoke before he had the chance.

"*Chop?* I was thinking more along the lines of the tree lot near the center of town." She placed one hand on her belly. "I don't think I'm up to much more than that."

"Tell you what," he said, unwilling to give up on

the Currier and Ives image in his head. "If I promise you won't have to chop anything, not even so much as an onion, will you go to the mountains with me? Just the two of us. We can ask someone to stay with your grandfather if it would ease your mind."

For several heartbeats, she said nothing. Then that soft, pleased smile of hers returned, gently curving the corners of her mouth.

"Okay, Joe, I'll go with you. If that's what you want."

Chapter Fourteen

Alicia awakened early the next morning, feeling as excited as a child. She'd actually dreamed about being in the mountains with Joe, watching him chopping down tall trees. The dream had been so real she would have sworn she could smell the scent of pine in the room.

A whole day alone with Joe. It sounded wonderful.

But she didn't allow herself to read more into it than what was on the surface. She was going to savor every moment and be thankful for it. She was going to love him with all her heart. But she wasn't going to ask more from him than what he freely offered.

Beside her, Rosie stirred, meowed, stretched, then climbed onto Alicia's lap—what there was of it. Seconds later Rags plopped her muzzle onto the mattress and whined softly.

"Morning, Rags," she whispered as she patted the dog's head.

"Everybody's awake, huh?"

Her heart fluttered at the sound of Joe's sleep-filled, slightly grumpy voice.

"I'm sorry," she said. "Did we wake you?"

"No." The springs of the sofa bed squeaked as he sat up. "Mind if I take a shower first?"

Rags left her bedside and trotted across the room to check on Joe.

"No. Go ahead. I can wait."

Joe spoke softly to the dog, something that sounded a lot like "dumb mutt." Then he rose and went into the bathroom. Before closing the door, he said, "Make sure Rosie stays with you."

Alicia smiled as she stroked the cat's fur. "Poor Joe. You've got him terrorized, my precious."

She listened to the sounds coming from the other side of the bathroom door. The toilet flushing. Joe brushing his teeth. Water running. The shower door opening and closing.

How very familiar those sounds were to her now. How very *married* they made her feel.

If things were different—

She stopped the thought before it could fully form. She'd already determined not to go down that path again.

"Sorry, Rosie," she said as she gently swept the cat from her lap.

She got up, switched on her bedside lamp, then made her bed. Just as she plumped the last pillow and dropped it into place, the bathroom door opened and

Joe came out—shirtless, clad in jeans, his feet bare, rubbing his hair with a towel.

She almost laughed, struck suddenly by the absurdity of her situation. She was living with the most gorgeous male she'd ever seen. He was sleeping in her bedroom and walking around half-dressed in front of her. They were legally married. He stirred feelings in her heart and body unlike anything she'd felt before. And yet they'd shared nothing more intimate than a kiss.

Come to think of it, maybe she would rather cry than laugh.

"Have you seen my brush?" he asked, intruding on her thoughts. "It isn't on the counter or in the drawer."

"No, I haven't seen it." She gave her head a slight shake, both answering his question *and* clearing her thoughts.

"Care if I use yours?"

"Go ahead."

"Can't figure it out," he said, more to himself than to her, as he turned back into the bathroom. "I never used to lose things."

While Joe finished in the bathroom, Alicia made up the sofa bed, destroying all evidence of their continued sleeping arrangements. That, too, struck her as slightly amusing. All over the world, there were girls and women keeping secrets about who they *were* going to bed with. And there she was, hiding who she was *not* sleeping with—her own husband!

"I would've done that," Joe said from behind her.

She turned. He was standing closer than she'd expected, and her heart responded to him in its usual erratic manner, making it difficult to draw a steady breath.

He took the blankets from her arms. "From now on, you leave this to me. You shouldn't be doing all that bending and pulling." He pointed toward the bathroom. "Hurry and get ready. I'll fix breakfast."

"I haven't checked on Grandpa—"

"Go on. I'll do it."

Fifteen days. She could let herself believe this was real for fifteen more days.

Joe had been a teenager the last time he'd driven this highway through the mountains to Idaho City. It had been winter then, too, and he and a bunch of his friends, as many as they could pack into one vehicle, had spent the day tubing at the gulch, followed by a swim at the hot springs. If memory served, his driving was more conservative on this trip than on the last.

"You're grinning," Alicia said. "What's funny?"

He released a low chuckle. "I was thinking what a miracle it is that anybody grows older than sixteen."

The words were scarcely out of his mouth when a souped-up, low-slung automobile came barreling up the road behind him. The driver, male, under twenty and stupid, laid on the horn, then passed Joe's SUV seconds before the road curved sharply to the right. Alicia gasped as the car fishtailed before disappearing from view.

"See what I mean?" Joe grumbled.

She made no reply, but he sensed her tension. He let up on the gas pedal, hoping to reassure her.

"Were you a reckless teenager?" she asked after a lengthy period of silence.

"Reckless enough."

"I don't remember that about you. You seemed so grown-up, so responsible and mature. You were always doing nice things for Belinda."

"Not always." He tried to remember the last time he'd talked to his sister. Too long, that was for certain. "I was as ornery to her as my mom let me get away with."

"I envied Belinda her big brother. I knew she never got lonely the way I did."

He cast a quick glance in her direction. "Were you lonely a lot?"

"Oh, I don't suppose you could call it a lot. But sometimes…"

He wished he remembered the child she'd been better than he did; the memories were fuzzy at best. She'd been a little girl of ten, skinny, freckled, hair worn in twin braids down her back. His little sister's friend.

At seventeen, the only girls he'd noticed were the ones with big breasts and tight jeans, preferably with hormones racing as fast as his own.

"You're grinning again," she accused.

This time his laugh was boisterous.

"What?"

"I think I'll take the Fifth this time," he said, still chuckling. "I want you speaking to me when we get to Idaho City."

"Hmm."

Her murmur of suspicion only made his grin broaden.

"Humphrey Harris," she said in a stage whisper, "no matter how many little brothers or sisters you have, you must promise not to be as ornery to them as Joe was to Belinda."

He felt a peculiar flash of disappointment when she used the name Harris with Humphrey, but he decided he'd rather not analyze why. At least not right now.

"Oh, look!" Alicia's hand lightly touched his right arm. "Joe, slow down. Look up there. On your left."

He followed her commands and saw a small herd of elk on the hillside. The bull raised its head to stare at the highway.

Joe whistled beneath his breath. "Holy frijoles! Look at the rack on that fellow." He pulled to the side of the road and stopped.

"Isn't he magnificent?" she whispered.

"Sure is. Think of the hunting seasons he's made it through unscathed. He's gotta be old to have that many points."

"Are you a hunter?" She didn't sound accusatory, only curious.

He shrugged. "Some. Never seem to have enough time. But I enjoy a good elk steak when I can get it."

"Well, I'm glad no hunter's shot that one."

"Me, too." He looked at Alicia. "Because then I couldn't have shared him with you."

They reached Idaho City before eleven. Not unexpectedly, the streets in this former gold rush town in the central Idaho mountains were quiet. Tomorrow, a Saturday, would be different. Folks from the valley would come up for trees or sledding, cross-country skiing, snowmobiling or a relaxing swim at the warm springs. But today it was mostly locals whose four-wheel-drive vehicles were parked in front of the local business establishments, few as they were.

"Where to now?" Alicia asked.

She leaned closer to the window and looked at the high walls of dirty snow the plows had left on either side of the road. It was difficult to see most of the buildings because of it.

"The paper said I could get directions at the Gold Bar Saloon."

"Not the ranger station?"

"You know how it is in these small towns. Nobody does things the way you expect." Joe turned off the main drag and slowed to a mere crawl. "There it is."

The Gold Bar Saloon was not much more than a large, faded sign and a false storefront. Judging by its exterior, it had to be one of the surviving buildings from the late 1800s.

Joe parked his vehicle in front of the saloon. "Need to use the rest room?"

"Yes. I'd better." She pressed a hand into the small of her back. "Besides, I need to stretch a bit."

"Sit tight. I'll come around for you."

Alicia smiled to herself. She had to admit. This sort of service was one of the few perks of being pregnant. Even men who would never otherwise *think* of opening a door for a woman had been opening her doors for the past couple of months. They also pulled out chairs and allowed her to move ahead in a line.

She was going to miss the many small courtesies once they stopped.

Joe opened the passenger side door and said, "Here we go."

She took hold of his hand, and he helped her safely to the ground. Immediately he took hold of her arm with a firm grasp. She'd grown to like that, too, Joe walking close, protecting her.

Once inside the dilapidated building, Joe paused to let their eyes adjust to the dim light. Then he said, "There's the rest room. You go ahead. I'll get directions and meet you back here."

She didn't argue with him, suddenly in a hurry, in the way of all expectant mothers. But hurrying didn't turn out to be an easy thing. Not dressed as she was in several layers of clothes. Why on earth had she purchased a pair of bibbed maternity ski pants? She couldn't imagine what had possessed her.

As she reached beneath her oversize sweater and bulky down coat to release the straps from their clasps, she caught sight of herself in the mirror. No one *that* big should have to go through such crazy gyrations, she thought. And then she chuckled. At this rate she would still be in the rest room an hour from now.

What was keeping her? Joe wondered. If she didn't speed things up, they were going to miss their scheduled departure to the lodge. He glanced at his watch again, then back at the rest room door.

"Come on, Alicia," he muttered. "Get a move on."

As if on cue, the door opened, and out she came, smiling as if someone had told her a joke.

"Ready?"

She arched an eyebrow at his impatient tone. Her

smile faded. "Why? Are the trees going some-where?"

"No." *Darn!* He wanted to keep it a secret a little longer. "Guess I'm afraid Christmas will get here before we're ready." He took hold of her arm. "Can't let that happen."

"Do we have time for me to get something to drink? I was hoping—"

"I think there's a store up the road a ways. We'll stop there."

"But I'm thirsty. Can't I—"

He pretended not to hear. He steered her out the saloon doorway, to his vehicle and into the passenger seat. When he settled behind the wheel, he could feel her staring at him in confusion. He didn't return the look. He was afraid he would spoil the surprise if he did.

He pulled onto the street. When he reached the highway, he turned north again, heading higher into the mountains. They drove in silence, and he assumed she was mad at him for refusing to get her something to drink. He wouldn't blame her if she was. But what choice had he had? They were cutting it close as it was.

The road curved, and suddenly there was a huge sign. Christmas Sleigh Rides, it proclaimed. A red arrow guided him to a parking lot cut out of the forest.

"Joe?"

He dared to glance her way as the SUV rolled to a stop.

"Merry Christmas, Alicia."

He would have been hard-pressed to describe what the look in her eyes made him feel.

"Oh, Joe."

"Surprised?"

"Yes." There were tears in her eyes and the brightest of smiles on her mouth.

Then he knew what he felt like…like somebody's hero. Like *Alicia's* hero.

"I thought we were getting a tree?" she said softly.

"We are." He shut off the engine, unfastened his seat belt and opened his door. "A tree and a whole lot more. Come on. You'll see."

It was one of the best days of her life.

Three couples and the driver rode in a bright red sleigh that was pulled by a pair of draft horses with thick winter coats and flowing manes and tails. The steady but muffled beat of their hooves matched the rhythm of jingling bells on the rigging. Otherwise, the snow-covered mountains were eerily silent.

Beneath a layer of plaid woolen blankets, Alicia snuggled against Joe's side, enjoying the passing countryside almost as much as the feel of his arm around her shoulders.

She couldn't get over that he'd done this for her. That he'd plotted and planned, keeping it a secret. She had to remind herself to simply enjoy it. To not make Joe's surprise into more than he'd intended it to be.

"Warm enough?" he asked her.

"Yes." But she snuggled closer, anyway.

"Look over there, folks."

Alicia reluctantly moved her head from Joe's shoulder, following the driver's outstretched arm with her gaze. She was just in time to see a fox darting across a clearing, a reddish-brown blur against the white landscape.

"He's not the only one looking for something to eat," the driver said, pointing again, this time upward.

"What is it?" the woman directly behind Alicia asked.

"Prairie falcon."

The bird soared elegantly, effortlessly, as if it were suspended from heaven itself.

"He's takin' it easy right now," the driver continued. "But falcons have been known to dive at over two-hundred miles an hour. Pesticides and spreadin' cities have about killed 'em off, but they're makin' a comeback. If you've never been, you ought to visit the Birds of Prey Reserve down on the Snake River."

In a low voice Joe said, "Seeing something that beautiful tends to make a person thankful to be alive. Doesn't it?"

"Yes." She glanced at him. "Thank you, Joe."

He smiled, then he kissed her forehead. "I'm having a good time, too."

The driver interrupted again. "We'll be to the lodge soon. It's around the next bend."

Alicia was sorry to hear it. She didn't care if this ride never ended.

As if he'd read her thoughts, Joe tightened his arm and said, "The day's not over yet."

Chapter Fifteen

The focal point of the lodge's cavernous main room was a stone fireplace, appropriately large enough to heat the room. A blazing fire on the grate greeted the cold but cheerful group when they entered the lodge.

Like the others with her, Alicia looked around, delighted by everything she saw.

The hardwood floor was scuffed and scratched, worn from years of use. Rustic log beams ran the length of the ceiling. Near the center of the room, three round tables had been set with red tablecloths, white tapers in crystal candle holders, and plates with a pattern of holly and mistletoe painted around the edges. A pair of Christmas trees, draped with garlands of red and green and silver, added to the festive decor. Familiar carols played softly over loudspeakers decorated with tinsel and candy canes, and delicious odors wafted from the adjoining kitchen area.

Joe leaned close to Alicia. "Notice how they've placed those Christmas trees. You can't see the other tables. They're giving each couple their privacy."

His warm breath on her neck caused goose pimples to rise on her arm.

"Hope you like barbecue," he added.

"I do."

"It seems more of a summertime offering to me, but I guess it goes with the surroundings."

She looked at him. "It's perfect. Everything's perfect."

His grin made it even more so.

A large man—easily six foot four, with a girth that nearly matched his height—came through a pair of swinging doors from the kitchen, a Santa hat perched on his head.

"Welcome, folks. Come on in. Come on in." He motioned with his hands. "That's right. Take yourselves over by the fire and get warm. I'm Harold, owner of the Nugget Lodge. This here's my wife, Marisa."

A woman about half her husband's size stepped from behind him, flashing a bright smile at one and all. She was wearing a Santa hat, too.

"You just give your coats to Marisa," Harold continued, "and then make yourselves at home. We'll have your dinners out in no time. Sure hope you're hungry." With that he turned and strode into the kitchen.

Marisa came forward with an outstretched arm. "Let me take your coats. Did you stay warm enough in the sleigh? Did you see any deer? How about elk?

See any of them?'' She kept talking without giving anyone a chance to answer her questions.

Alicia exchanged an amused glance with Joe as she handed her coat to the woman.

''Well, look at you!'' Marisa exclaimed. ''About ready to pop, ain't you? When's that baby due?'' Finally, an expectant pause.

''Next month,'' Alicia replied softly.

Marisa patted Alicia's tummy, then looked at Joe. ''You're one lucky man. You take good care of this pretty little mama now.'' She winked at him, then moved off toward the other couples.

''Friendly, isn't she?'' Joe asked in a low voice.

''Very.'' She met his gaze again, relieved to see the humor in his eyes. ''Isn't it the Buddha's belly you're supposed to rub for good luck? Well, that's how I feel sometimes.''

Joe put one arm around her shoulders, then laid his other hand on the exact same spot Marisa had patted a few moments before. ''Here's to good luck. For both of us.''

Was it possible Alicia had grown prettier over the weeks he'd been living with her? Joe wondered.

Firelight flickered across her features and streaked her hair with gold. There was a pretty peach-pink flush in her cheeks and a soft upward curve in the corners of her mouth. Her eyes had turned from aquamarine to midnight-blue in the dimly lit room.

He might have kissed her if the proprietor hadn't poked his head out of the kitchen at that precise moment and announced they should all be seated.

Maybe it was just as well.

The barbecued beef, the garlic mashed potatoes, the

salads and breads and other side dishes were all delicious. Even better than the article in the paper had described. But it was Joe's charming companion, his temporary wife, who made the meal seem like the best he'd ever eaten.

Their conversation centered on childhood Christmases, on memories of other trips to the mountains to ski or sled or visit the hot springs that were in abundance in this area. Alicia told Joe about the time she broke her thumb while sledding on a hillside above Lucky Peak Reservoir. He told her about the time he flew over the moguls at Bogus Basin and crashed—*spectacularly* crashed, he was quick to point out—right in front of the beginners' class by the rope tow. She told him about the Christmas she got a puppy named Rags, a gift from her grandfather. He told her about the year he gave his sister a black eye during a childhood squabble and had to spend the entire Christmas break in his room.

Over dessert—spice cake with cream cheese frosting—she expressed the loneliness of recent holidays. Somewhat surprised by his own admission, he said the same was true for him. Only he'd always been too busy to recognize it.

"We won't be lonely this year," she said in a near whisper.

"No. Not this year."

But what about next year? he wondered.

Joe might have voiced his question aloud if Harold hadn't returned and announced that the sleigh was waiting to take them to chop down their trees.

"Your coats and things are next to the door." He pointed. "When you're done, Gus will bring you back here for hot chocolate or coffee before you head down to the parking lot.'' Harold waved a farewell, then retreated to the kitchen once again.

"Gus," Alicia said as she looked at Joe. "I wondered what our driver's name was." She smiled, a twinkle in her eyes. "He even looks like a Gus, doesn't he?"

Joe couldn't say he'd given any thought to what a "Gus" was supposed to look like, but he nodded anyway.

"I'd better use the rest room before we go." She rose from her chair. "Don't let the sleigh leave without me."

"I won't."

She waddled away, and Joe couldn't help grinning as he watched her. After all, she looked adorable.

It took about twenty minutes to reach the tree farm.

Gus brought the sleigh to a halt, then twisted on the driver's seat and said, "Spruce trees are over that way." He pointed. "And the ponderosa pines are over that way." He moved his arm in another direction. "Signs are clearly marked. Trees range from four to eight feet. If you need help, all you need do is ask."

Joe waited until the other couples had disembarked, then he asked Alicia, "Do you want to stay in the sleigh?"

"Not on your life. I want the full experience."

"Okay, but you hang on to me. I don't want you falling."

She was happy to oblige. Holding on to Joe was her favoritemost thing to do...except for kissing him.

"Which type of Christmas tree do you prefer?" he asked as he helped her to the ground.

"Spruce."

"Okay." He selected an ax from the rear of the sleigh. Then, holding it in his right hand, he offered her his left arm. "Let's go."

The trails had been well packed, and walking was easier than Alicia had expected it to be. Their boots only made slight impressions in the snow. Still, Joe's pace was slow in deference to her condition.

No wonder I love him, she thought, casting a surreptitious glance in his direction.

He wore no hat, and the tops of his ears were red with the cold. His thick black hair was delightfully windblown from the sleigh ride. She could see a faint blue-black shadow beneath his skin. In another five hours his cheek would be prickly with a beard's stubble, but for now it would be smooth to the touch.

Joe stopped walking. "How about that one?" He indicated a tree with his outstretched arm.

She looked, although she'd truly forgotten they were there for a tree until he reminded her.

"What do you think?" he asked. "Put it in the alcove next to the piano. It'll pretty much fill up the window space there."

"I love it. It's perfect."

No point in telling him she wanted whatever he wanted. If he'd picked a scraggly pine with needles falling off, she would have said it was perfect.

He grinned. "Okay. You stand right here, Ms. Harris, and watch a man do his work." With an exaggerated John Wayne swagger, he walked away from her, the ax handle now resting on his shoulder.

She laughed aloud. "My hero."

"You mock me?" He glanced back at her.

"Never!"

"Good."

He walked around the selected tree, inspecting it. Alicia knew the tree was tall—at least seven feet— and full, but she was inspecting Joe, not the tree.

Falling in love, her grandfather had once told her, was an emotion, a roller-coaster ride that happened to you. But being in love, staying in love, loving in sickness, in health, and in whatever other circumstances life brought, was a decision made daily. "God wouldn't have told us to love our spouses," he'd said, "if we couldn't *choose* to love them, even when they're at their least lovable."

That's how I want to love you, Joe. Not just now when looking at you makes my heart race, but when we're both old and gray. I want to choose to love you every morning of my life.

"Okay," he called to her. "Here goes."

He took his first swing. The sound of metal striking wood rang in the forest. He swung again, and wood chips flew through the air. He paused, removed his gloves and shucked off his bulky down coat, then began wielding the ax again.

The rhythm of Joe's movements resonated in Alicia's chest. Back swing. Forward swing. *Crack!* Back swing. Forward swing. *Crack!*

She cupped her hands around her mouth and shouted, "You could do this professionally."

He paused, looked her way, grinned. "Maybe I'll give up practicing law and buy a tree farm like this one. What would you think of that? A lodge in the mountains where the snowdrifts pile six or ten feet deep in the winter months and elk come to forage in the front yard?''

Her heart fluttered. Was he including her in that fantasy? All she could do was smile and nod.

Joe was enjoying this more than he'd imagined he would. When the tree toppled, accompanied by a loud *crack* as the trunk splintered in two, he stared at the fruit of his labor with satisfaction. But before he could see if Alicia was suitably impressed, something cold and wet hit the side of his head.

''What the—?''

Her laughter rang all around him.

He touched his head. Snow? A snowball! She'd thrown a snowball at him!

He turned. She was watching him with wide eyes, trying hard to look innocent.

It didn't work.

''Not a wise thing to do, my dear,'' he said, bending down to grab a handful of the white stuff.

''You wouldn't throw a snowball at a pregnant woman, would you?''

He revealed what he hoped was a wicked grin. ''You're about to find out.''

She turned and started away from him as quickly as she could. He might have thought she was afraid, only he heard her laughter again. He took off in pursuit, part of him enjoying the chase, part of him worried about her slipping and falling.

She couldn't hope to outdistance him, and he caught up with her in short order. His hand on her arm stayed her flight. An instant later, he had her wrapped in a tight embrace.

"Foolish woman. I may not pay you back now, but it'll snow again next year. You won't be pregnant then." Too late, he realized what his words implied.

Silence encompassed them. Alicia's blue-green eyes swirled with emotions Joe would just as soon not recognize. He could almost hear her heart beating, almost grasp the breathless anticipation of the moment.

"You confuse the heck out of me," he whispered, his mouth drawing closer to hers.

"I'm sorry, Joe. That's not my intent."

Even more softly, he said, "I know. That only makes it worse."

He kissed her, long and slow and sweet. Their mingled breaths formed a misty cloud above their heads.

Time stood still.

Joe knew he was treading on dangerous ground. He knew he shouldn't be holding her, kissing her, enjoying her, caring about her. He knew he was all wrong for her. He was all wrong for any woman. He was definitely all wrong for marriage. There was no future for them, and it would be unfair to let either of them think otherwise.

He drew back, no more than an inch. He planned to tell her again all the reasons why they shouldn't do this. But when he opened his eyes, he found her watching him, and the look she gave him stole the words straight out of his head.

He couldn't think. All he could do was kiss her again.

Alicia allowed hope to return. Her heart soared with it. Her mind sang with it. It pulsed through her veins like lifeblood itself.

When Joe pulled away a second time, his expression was both grim and puzzled. He searched her face with his gaze; she tried to hide what she felt for him by looking away.

"We'd better get back to the sleigh," he said. "The others will be waiting for us."

"Yes," she whispered.

"I'll get the tree."

"Okay."

"Can you carry the ax?"

"I'm not a weakling."

"I just don't want to take chances."

She glanced at him again. "I know." She felt dangerously close to tears.

He turned on his heel and strode across the snow to where he'd dropped the ax. He picked it up and brought it to her, passing it into her waiting hands without a word. Then he returned to the felled tree. He put on his coat and gloves, keeping his back toward Alicia the entire time. Finally he grasped the tree trunk with both hands and began dragging it in her direction.

"Watch your step," he said as he drew near. "I'll be right behind you."

Why did love have to be so hard? she wondered as she turned toward the sleigh. Why couldn't Joe love her simply because she loved him?

The memory of his kisses flowed over her, causing her knees to weaken. She stumbled slightly.

"Alicia?"

She raised one hand but didn't look back. "I'm fine." She kept walking.

Love, she decided, was always hard.

Chapter Sixteen

It was after five o'clock by the time Joe pulled his vehicle into the driveway.

After he'd turned the key and the engine fell silent, Alicia said, "Would you mind if we wait to decorate the tree until tomorrow? I'm exhausted."

"No, I don't mind. If that's what you want."

She opened the passenger door. "It is." She stepped down to the sidewalk, shoveled clear of snow. Then she looked back at him. "Thanks for the wonderful day, Joe. I'll remember it always."

"Sure thing."

He frowned as he watched her walk toward the back porch, a hand in the small of her back. Maybe he shouldn't have taken her up there. Maybe she'd done too much.

But deep down, he knew that wasn't what was bothering her.

And it sure as heck wasn't what was bothering *him*!

No, it was those blasted kisses they'd exchanged while standing in that grove of trees. It was the dreamy, faraway look in her eyes when they'd parted. It was the way her cologne lingered in his nostrils and the taste of her mouth lingered on his tongue.

Muttering a few choice words beneath his breath, he got out of the vehicle. When he entered the kitchen, he found Grandpa Roger seated at the table, a steaming bowl of stew in front of him, along with a loaf of home-baked bread.

Joe acknowledged him with a nod, then glanced toward the doorway to the living room.

"She went to bed," her grandfather said.

"Maybe this wasn't such a good idea, going up there."

"She told me she had a wonderful time."

Joe looked toward the elderly man but didn't reply.

"There's more stew on the stove." Grandpa Roger motioned toward it. "A friend of mine made it and the bread. You're welcome to help yourself. It's good."

"I should check on Alicia first. I'll be back."

Moments later he looked into the bedroom and found her already in bed, the blankets pulled almost over her head. Her maternity wear—bibbed ski pants and oversize slipover sweater—had been dropped on a chair, and her boots and socks had been set beneath it.

For someone who'd complained about the difficulty of dressing and undressing, she'd done an admirable—and quick—job of it.

He stepped back and closed the door, then returned

to the kitchen. A place had been set for him at the table, and he joined Alicia's grandfather there.

"So tell me what all you did?" Grandpa Roger encouraged him.

It was easier to talk about the day's activities than to think about his feelings for Alicia, so Joe was willing to oblige the old man. He talked about the wildlife they'd seen, about the sleigh ride, about the lodge and its proprietor and his wife, about the tree farm, even about the snowball Alicia had thrown at him.

And when he'd run out of things to say, he asked, "What did you do all day, sir?"

"Took it easy." Grandpa Roger scooted his chair back from the table, then reached into the pocket of his sweater vest. "I have something for you." He withdrew a blue velvet box from his pocket and set it on the table. "Open it."

Joe picked it up. He cast a questioning glance at the old man.

"Go on. Open it."

He obeyed, lifting the lid to reveal an antique pocket watch. The gold hunting case bore the image of an elk, intricately etched into the surface. Time had smoothed the craftsman's work but not destroyed it.

"It was my grandfather's. Then it was my father's. Then it was mine. Then it was my son's."

Joe removed it from the box and opened the case.

"Cost more than forty dollars. That was a lot of money in its day. Twenty ruby jewels in gold settings, Breguet hairspring, double-sunk dial, fourteen-karat-gold-filled case. It came with a twenty-year guarantee. Still runs, too, when the stem is wound."

"It's great, sir." Joe looked from the watch in his hand to the elderly man.

"It's for you to give to your son."

A lump formed in Joe's throat, and he had to look away.

"It's tradition for it to go to the firstborn male in each generation. I was going to give it to Alicia to keep until she has a son the right age, but…well, now that you're part of the family, I'd like you to hang on to it."

"And if this baby isn't a boy?"

Grandpa Roger laughed. "Well, there comes a time when even good traditions should be broken. Probably should have gone to Alicia when she turned eighteen. You can give it to your daughter, if that's what you choose. Just keep it in the family. That's all I ask. A reminder of those who've gone before."

Joe was an impostor. He had no right to be holding this family heirloom.

"Don't tell Alicia I gave it to you, though," her grandfather continued. "She'll see it as some sort of sign that I think I'm dying. You've seen how she frets over me."

"Yes, sir."

Grandpa Roger reached forward and touched Joe's hand, forcing him to look up. "I thought we'd settled this 'sir' business. I'm supposed to be Grandpa to you by now."

"Tough habit to break." He shrugged, offering a weak smile at the same time. "Always called my dad sir, too."

"Well, see if you can't manage to break the habit before I head back to Arizona." Grandpa Roger rose with a soft groan. "Wouldn't think I'd be so tired after doing nothing all day, but I am. I'm turning in." He reached for his bowl and empty milk glass.

"Just leave the dishes. I'll take care of them."

"Thanks, my boy."

Long after Grandpa Roger had left the kitchen, Joe sat staring at the watch and wondering how he would feel if he really were the baby's father.

Although Alicia was forced by her condition to get up frequently in the night, it wasn't until she awakened early the next morning that she realized Joe hadn't slept on the sofa bed.

She tried not to feel alarmed. After all, there was no rule that said he *had* to share her bedroom. But it worried her, anyway.

As soon as she finished in the bathroom, she went looking for him. He was in the basement, asleep in his makeshift office, his head cradled on his arms atop his desk.

"Joe?" She touched his shoulder.

He awakened slowly, blinking his eyes, straightening with a groan, a look of confusion on his face.

"Did you stay down here all night?"

"I guess so." He glanced around the cramped room, as if making certain he knew where he was. "I must've fallen asleep while I was working."

Alicia didn't know whether to be disappointed or relieved.

Joe stretched, then yawned while scratching his head. "I got a letter from a law firm in Boise. I discovered it with the rest of the mail after your grandfather went to bed last night." He glanced toward his laptop. When he touched the pad, the black screen vanished, replaced by a day-planner program. "They want to meet with me next week. I was working on my portfolio and must've decided to rest my eyes. That's the last thing I remember."

"Are you pleased about it?"

"They're one of the top firms in Idaho. I'd be lucky to get on with them."

Alicia sat on the chair on the opposite side of the desk, pulling her robe closed over her stomach. "They'd be the lucky ones."

"You're prejudiced."

I'm supposed to be. I'm your wife.

More awake now, he gave her a tender smile. "You always look cute in the mornings. You know that?"

"Don't be silly," she replied, flustered by the unexpected compliment. She pushed her tousled hair away from her face with one hand. "I'm a sight."

"I think it's those bunny slippers." He rose and peered over the desk at her feet. When he sat down again, he said, "Yup, it's those slippers that make you so darn cute."

Her heart performed crazy palpitations in response to his teasing words.

"If you'll tell me where you keep your Christmas decorations, we can decorate the tree after I have my coffee." He yawned and stretched again. "Only a week left until Christmas. No time to waste."

One week until Christmas. Two weeks until her grandfather returned to Arizona. And then Joe would leave, too.

How she wished she could make time stand still.

"Alicia? The decorations?"

She stood as quickly as she was able. "In the storage closet at the foot of the stairs. The boxes are clearly marked." She turned toward the door. "I'll start the coffee brewing."

"This is one of my personal favorites," Grandpa Roger said, holding out an ornament for Joe to see. "Alicia made this at Sunday School when she was about seven or eight."

Joe took the shellacked, walnut half-shell ornament. Inside was a miniature doll covered by a piece of burlap. It looked like a baby in a cradle. On the bottom, in tiny lettering—obviously not that of a child—had been painted "John 3:16." Gold thread was attached at both ends so it could be hung on a tree.

"It's meant to be baby Jesus in the manger," Grandpa Roger finished.

Joe stared into the box on the table. "Looks like making decorations was an annual pastime."

"It was." Alicia came to stand beside him. "My mom was very crafty."

"So that's where you got it."

She raised an eyebrow in question.

Joe motioned with an arm. "Your entire house is filled with those little touches." He lowered his voice. "The kind of things that make a place feel like a home."

An attractive flush rose in her cheeks.

His throat felt tight as he added, "I never paid much attention to that kind of stuff before I came here."

She smiled, a look as warm and comforting as the home she'd made for herself.

He thought about kissing her.

Then he thought better of it.

As if sensing his decision, she returned to the box Joe had placed on the sofa. "Remember bubble lights?" she asked, lifting a string of them. "I think these are older than I am."

"They most certainly are," her grandfather interjected. "Teresa bought those when your father was just a boy. My goodness. How very long ago that was. Do they still work?"

Alicia plugged them into the outlet, and they all lit up. "They do," she answered, looking and sounding as excited as a child. "Watch and see how long it takes for them to start bubbling."

She would be the sort of mother who made Christmas special for her children, Joe thought, looking at her, rather than the lights. She would bake cookies and build snowmen. She would hide wrapped packages all over the house. She would tell her children bedtime stories, and she would probably be as sleepless as the little ones on Christmas Eve.

Joe's mother hadn't made cookies or snowmen, hadn't hidden packages, hadn't told bedtime stories. He supposed she had done the best she could, but her loneliness had affected the way she approached the holidays. He couldn't remember a Christmas his dad hadn't gone to his office for at least part of the day. Of course, there'd been plenty of toys and other presents. That's how his mother had tried to make up for everything else that was lacking.

But Alicia's baby would have different memories.

Lucky kid.

Joe looked across the room, watched as Alicia began stringing lights on the tree. She moved somewhat awkwardly, her extended belly often in the way. It made Joe smile, thinking again how cute she looked.

A very lucky kid.

Decorating the Christmas tree had been an event in her parents' home, and Alicia had tried to continue the tradition, even in the years when she'd been alone for the holidays. But this Christmas she was with Grandpa and Joe. That made it even more special.

They paused often in their decorating to reminisce. Almost every ornament had a memory tied to it. Grandpa Roger was a superb storyteller, and he was in his element today, regaling them with one tale after another. He seemed to take particular pleasure in telling Joe about Alicia's childhood escapades.

She lost track of the number of times Joe's gaze met with hers. Each time it happened, her pulse skittered, then raced. It was obvious she'd failed in her effort to think of him as merely a friend. She might not be allowed to tell him she loved him, but her heart wasn't fooled. Not for a moment.

When they were finished, the last ornament in place atop the tree, the three of them stood back, Alicia between the two men, and admired their handiwork.

"I don't believe I've seen a better tree in all my born days," Grandpa Roger said with the voice of authority.

"I think maybe you're right." Joe slipped his arm around Alicia's shoulders.

Alicia could only smile in pure, unadulterated bliss.

"You know what we need now?" Her grandfather looked at her. "Hot, spiced apple cider."

"Oh, Grandpa, how could I forget? I'll have to run to the store."

"No, you won't," he said. "I had Joe pick up everything we need last week."

"You did?"

Joe squeezed her shoulders. "Cider. Cinnamon sticks. Cloves, I think. Was there something else?" He turned toward the kitchen, steering her with him. "Come on. I'll help you."

Happiness flowed through her, warm and inviting. She would treasure the memory of this day for the rest of her life.

Her vision blurred, but she managed to reply in a fairly normal voice, "Great. I'd love your help."

While Alicia retrieved a large pot from the cupboard near the stove, Joe brought a paper grocery bag in from the back porch.

"I've got a gallon of cider. Want the whole thing in there?"

"Please," she answered.

As he poured the golden brown liquid into the pot, Joe said, "I meant to tell you. I hired someone to come in next week and finish the nursery wallpapering." He glanced at her. "No comment?"

She smiled. "No comment."

"Good."

Alicia turned on the electric burner beneath the pot, then added several cinnamon sticks to the cider.

"I bet you'll be glad when the waiting is over."

"Waiting?"

"For the baby to be born."

His comment surprised her, but she tried not to show it. "These last weeks have seemed awfully long."

"You've never said if you want a boy or a girl."

"Yes." She smiled. "I want a boy or a girl."

He chuckled. "I walked into that one, didn't I?"

"Uh-huh."

"You must have decided on everything you want for the nursery by now. When do you plan to set up the room?"

It was the sort of conversation Alicia imagined any expectant couple might have while they stood together in the kitchen. His words made her heart flutter with happiness; she yearned for it to be real.

"Soon," she answered, hoping her emotions weren't revealed in her voice. "Everything's in stock except for the cradle I want. The supplier promised he'll be able to deliver it by mid-January. That should be in time. First babies often come late."

"I didn't know that." He spoke softly. "But then, I didn't know much about babies before I was married to you."

Their gazes met and held for a heartbeat.

She thought he might say more.

He remained silent.

"How's that cider coming?" Grandpa Roger called from the other room.

The moment was lost.

Alicia looked toward the stove. "It needs to simmer at least an hour to be good, Grandpa."

"You know—" Joe cleared his throat as he took a step back from the counter "—if it's going to be that long, I think I'll clear up some work on my desk, maybe check my e-mail. Call me when it's ready.''

''Okay.''

The kitchen felt much too large, much too empty after he left.

Joe didn't accomplish a thing. He spent the next hour staring at a blank computer screen and wondering what the heck was going on with him. He didn't know his own mind anymore, and that was an uncomfortable condition for his personality type. He'd always liked knowing what he wanted and then going after it. But now...

He was almost relieved when Alicia called down to him that the spiced cider was ready.

He rolled the chair back from the desk and started to rise. He wasn't sure what caused him to glance at the top of the two-drawer filing cabinet beside the desk where his day planner should have been—and wasn't.

He frowned. What had he done with it? He checked in the corner behind him, then under the desk, then behind the open door. No sign of it.

''Maybe I put it in the bedroom,'' he muttered.

''Joe? Did you hear me? The cider's ready.''

''Coming.''

He swept the tiny office with his gaze one more time, as if hoping the day planner would suddenly and miraculously appear.

It didn't.

When he reached the kitchen, he asked Alicia, ''Have you seen my planner anywhere? About this big. Black cowhide.''

"Wasn't it next to your desk? I'm sure I saw it there this morning."

Joe's scowl deepened. "That's what I thought." He turned toward the living room. "I'm going to check in the bedroom."

He looked everywhere to no avail. It wasn't long before both Alicia and her grandfather were involved in the search, but they were no more successful than Joe had been. The day planner had vanished.

"Something's going on," he said to himself as he left the bedroom for the third time and walked down the hall toward the living room.

He found Alicia on her knees, looking behind the Christmas tree, her fanny stuck up in the air, her belly touching the floor, the ears of her pink bunny slippers flattened against the hardwood.

The sight made him chuckle.

She straightened, turning toward the sound. Joe fully expected a tongue-lashing for his humor at her expense, but instead, he heard a sharp gasp. A look of pain tightened her features.

He hurried across the room. "What's wrong?"

"I moved too fast is all. But I think I pulled a muscle in my back."

"You shouldn't have been down there in the first place." He took hold of both her arms and drew her to her feet.

A groan slipped from between her tightly pressed lips, although he could tell she'd done her best not to let it happen.

"You'd better lie down."

"The cider—" she began.

"The cider can wait. Come on."

As he turned her toward the bedroom, one arm around her back, the other holding her elbow, he discovered Grandpa Roger observing them from the kitchen doorway.

"I'm okay, Grandpa," Alicia said quickly.

The elderly man ignored her and asked Joe, "Should we call the doctor?"

"I don't know."

"Would you two listen to me?" Alicia exclaimed. "I'm okay. I just need a few minutes to rest."

"Stubborn, like your grandmother," Grandpa Roger retorted.

"More like my grandpa," she whispered so only Joe could hear.

He suppressed a smile and kept her moving toward the bedroom.

"This is *so* silly, Joe. I can see myself to bed."

"I don't mind. Besides, it's my fault you're in pain. If I hadn't misplaced my planner, you wouldn't have been on the floor like that."

They reached the side of the bed. Joe turned down the blankets and sheet, then plumped the pillows.

"Lie down and stay there until you feel better."

She tilted her head to one side and narrowed her eyes as she looked up at him. "You're getting mighty bossy, Mr. Palermo."

"You haven't begun to see how bossy I can be. You've been having twinges and pains for a couple of weeks now. You keep saying it's normal, but I'm not so sure. Come Monday, I think you'd better see your doctor."

She must have seen he meant business for she

sighed and nodded her head. "All right. I'll rest now, and next week is my checkup, anyway. Now go make sure Grandpa doesn't worry himself sick over this. It's nothing.''

Chapter Seventeen

The ache in Alicia's lower back came and went all the rest of the day. Sometimes it didn't feel like much. Other times it hurt like the dickens. But at least she convinced Joe and Grandpa Roger that she was feeling herself again.

Feeling herself.

When was the last time *that* had been an accurate description? She didn't know what "herself" should feel like.

Just what was normal? she wondered.

Much to her surprise and pleasure, Joe accompanied Alicia and Grandpa to church the following morning. She'd invited him before, but he'd always declined. She hadn't realized how much it would mean to her for him to say yes until it happened.

It began to snow again in the afternoon. Joe shoveled the walks three different times and spread ice melt as an extra safeguard. Alicia decided the least she could do was find his missing planner. However, there would be no more crawling on the floor.

Standing at the bottom of the stairs, she stared toward Joe's office. He wasn't a careless sort. On the contrary, he was well-organized. He wouldn't misplace his day planner. Since he'd come to live in her house, she'd seen him make numerous entries into that black book. She knew how important it was to him.

So what had happened to it? She couldn't imagine a thief coming into her home and stealing a planner while leaving a laptop and other valuables. No, there was no thief to blame. So who?

"Think," she said softly to herself.

Rosie rubbed against Alicia's shin, then serpentined between and around her ankles in two perfect figure eights.

"Sorry, girl. I'm too tired to bend over and pick you up."

Rosie meowed her complaint, then dashed up the stairs in a huff. Rags galloped out of the shadows at the opposite end of the basement. She whisked past Alicia in a blur of white and gray, playfully giving chase to the cat.

"Rags! Stop right now."

All Alicia needed was for those two to knock over the Christmas tree.

"*Sit!*"

The dog halted at the top of the stairs. She turned and plopped down on her back haunches, looking adorable...and totally unrepentant.

"Rags," Alicia began to scold.

And then she stopped.

Surely not.

She flipped one of the switches on the nearby wall. Bare bulbs cast an unforgiving light throughout the large main room of the basement. The floor was concrete, the walls plasterboarded but never finished out. Alicia rarely came down here. Until Joe set up his office in the room near the furnace, she'd had little reason to.

But Rags and Rosie had full run of the house, including the basement.

Alicia walked to the opposite end of the room. She couldn't believe what she found there. On an old, tattered blanket that the dog was obviously using for a bed, Alicia saw not only the remains of a day planner, but also Joe's missing hairbrush, pen and glove, plus some items he hadn't yet discovered were missing.

"Oh, Rags," Alicia whispered. "What have you done?"

With care, she bent down to pick up the binder. The expensive leather had been chewed like a rawhide toy. Pages had been ripped from the rings and were scattered everywhere. Some were so badly mauled there was no hope of knowing what had been written on them.

She heard the back door slam. Boots stomped on the floor overhead. Joe had finished shoveling the walks.

She closed her eyes. He'd never liked her animals. He barely tolerated them. Maybe it would be better if she didn't tell him what she'd found.

She released a sigh.

She had to tell him.

"No time like the present," she said aloud as she started up the stairs.

Joe placed the mug of spiced cider in the microwave, closed the door, and hit Start. The machine hummed for thirty seconds before he heard the familiar *ding*. But before he could retrieve his beverage, he heard the telltale squeak of the top step on the basement stairs. He looked over his shoulder.

Alicia's gaze met his, then dropped away.

Now what? he wondered. Living with her, it's always something.

"I found your planner."

"Where?"

She let out a breath, long and hopeless sounding. "Rags had it."

"Rags?"

She nodded before holding out his black binder.

It didn't look anything like what he'd lost.

"I'm so sorry, Joe." She straightened her arm, urging him to take the destroyed planner.

He opened the cover. The year's planning calendars were missing, as were several other sections.

"I guess she likes you," Alicia said softly.

"Likes me?"

"Your other things are down there, too."

"What other things?" The words were barely out of his mouth before he remembered—his pen, his glove, his brush. "Never mind."

"I *am* sorry. Rags didn't mean to do anything

wrong. I—'' She offered an anemic, beseeching smile. "I'm serious. I think she has a crush on you."

Dang pets! His thought was automatic, but after a moment he recognized it was only out of habit, not because he was angry or irritated. In fact, what he wanted to do was grin—so he did.

"Why don't you show me this evidence of your mutt's affection?"

She didn't say so, but he knew his lack of anger surprised her.

Almost as much as it surprised him.

Then he wondered what that said about him as a person. Not much, probably.

"Is it in the basement?" He motioned toward the stairs. "Might as well show me."

"You're not angry?"

"Surprised, huh?"

"Yes." Her reply was uncomfortably honest, but it came with another small smile.

"No more so than me."

Their gazes held a short while longer. Joe wondered what she was thinking behind those pretty aquamarine eyes of hers. He might have asked in a few more heartbeats, but she turned away and he lost his chance.

Rags seemed to know she'd stepped over some invisible line of acceptable behavior. For the remainder of the day she shadowed Joe, even going so far as to lay her head on his thigh while he sat at his desk, piecing together those planner pages that could be salvaged.

"I should wring your neck, you mangy no-good

hound,'' he told the dog—even as he stroked her head.

Rags whimpered.

''That's not going to get you any sympathy.''

How was it a dog could look repentant despite all that hair covering its eyes?

''What's happened to my life, Rags? Nothing's going the way it was supposed to. Nothing.''

He was still musing over his ever-surprising life later that evening. When the ten o'clock news broadcast was over, Grandpa Roger rose from the easy chair. ''I'm headed off to bed, you two. Good night.''

''Good night, Grandpa,'' Alicia responded. As the older man left the living room, she glanced at Joe who was seated on the sofa opposite her. ''I'm tired, too. Guess I'll turn in.''

It was all she could do to keep from adding, *Are you coming soon?* She couldn't ask it, of course. It sounded too ''married,'' and that was the last thing Joe wanted.

Pain stabbed her in the small of the back as she stood. She caught her breath in a gasp.

Joe's frown was instantaneous. ''Your back again?''

She nodded.

''You're going to the doctor's tomorrow.''

She didn't argue with him.

He turned off the television, then set aside the remote control and stood. ''You get into bed. I'll give you a back rub when you're ready. Maybe it'll help.''

Dumbfounded, she stared at him.

''Go on. I'll make sure all the doors are locked for the night. Won't take me long.''

She supposed it was possible she'd fallen asleep in her chair and was only dreaming. If so, she'd just as soon keep dreaming.

In the master bathroom she removed her clothes. Before dropping a maternity nightshirt over her head, she freshened her underarm deodorant and spritzed a little cologne onto her wrists. She brushed her teeth before gargling with mouthwash. A glance in the mirror told her it was useless to try to do anything with her hair.

Besides, it's only a dream.

A few moments later she crawled into bed, lying on her side. She waited...and waited...and waited. Maybe the dream was already over, she thought. Maybe he wasn't coming after all. But then he appeared in the bedroom doorway.

Their gazes met.

His smile was gentle.

Her reaction to it wasn't. It hit her right in the center of her heart; it filled her with a longing so great it was beyond description.

"Ready?" he asked, closing the door behind him. "Are you in a comfortable position?"

"I think so. As comfortable as I can get these days."

He switched off the overhead light, plunging the room into shades of gray and black, the only illumination provided by the nightlight. He went into the bathroom. She heard him opening and closing drawers and cabinets. Familiar sounds as he got ready for bed. About five minutes later he returned to the bedroom, carrying a flickering candle. He set it on the bedside stand.

A lit candle in an otherwise darkened bedroom seemed a romantic gesture. She knew she shouldn't think of it that way; she shouldn't even *want* it to be romantic. She would only be disappointed later.

Joe walked to the other side of the bed, out of her sight. The mattress shifted as he knelt on it. "I can't promise how effective this will be with you lying on your side. I'll do the best I can."

Breathless, she waited for his touch. When his fingers began to gently manipulate the muscles in her back, she closed her eyes, hoping she could memorize this moment. She wanted to be able to recall it, to treasure it in the years to come.

"Am I pressing too hard?"

She shook her head, unable to speak.

"You tell me if I do anything that causes discomfort."

"Okay," she managed to whisper.

He worked slowly. His hands were both skilled and gentle, and she relaxed beneath them. She was aware of nothing other than his nearness and the love for him that overflowed her heart.

A long while later he asked in a hushed voice, "Are you asleep?"

"No."

"Does your back feel better?" His hands stilled.

"Yes."

"Ready for me to stop?"

She released a whispery breath. "No."

He chuckled softly. "I think you're already falling asleep."

"Joe?" She opened her eyes, staring at the candlelight dancing on the wall, wishing she had the courage to roll onto her back and look at him.

"Hmm?"

"Hold me for a while. Stay with me."

Silence.

"Please. Just for one night."

More silence.

She expected him to move away from her. She expected him to rise from the bed, perhaps to leave the bedroom and sleep once again at his desk in the basement.

Eventually he did move away. But only for a moment. The candlelight vanished, the wick extinguished. And then, to her surprise, she felt him slip beneath the covers. He drew close to her again, his chest against her back, his arm draped over her side, hand resting on her belly.

Ecstasy and heartache warred inside her, the joy of the present and the dread of the future mingling together, creating emotional havoc. Tears slipped from her eyes to dampen her cheeks and pillow. She bit her lower lip; she prayed Joe wouldn't discover she wept.

Joe didn't know why he stayed when she asked him to. He didn't know why he chose to lie beside her, holding her spoonlike, allowing himself to be tortured by the subtle scent of her cologne.

The worst part was it felt right, being there. It felt good. He was tempted to kiss the nape of her neck. He was tempted to draw her closer.

The baby moved beneath his hand, reminding him that Alicia would be a mother in another month. Her house would be filled with crying and colic and diapers and 2:00 a.m. feedings. Chaos would reign supreme.

Rug rats and mogul monsters didn't fit into his long-term goals. Neither did a wife.

She's already my wife.

True, but only technically. That would be over soon. In a matter of weeks.

She said she loves me.

But they both knew it was gratitude she felt, not love. She hadn't said those words again because they hadn't been true.

But what if it is true? What if she does love me?

It wouldn't make a bit of difference. He still wouldn't stay with her. Not even if she loved him. Not even then. He couldn't.

Be a husband? Be a father? No. That wasn't for him.

Never had been.

Never would be.

He remembered his thoughts the day he'd arrived in Idaho: *undeniably, certifiably insane.* That description was as accurate now as it had been then.

No. He wouldn't stay with Alicia even if she loved him.

But what if I love her?

Alicia was surprised when she awakened to a bedroom flooded with daylight. She glanced at the clock. It was nearly ten-thirty. She couldn't believe she'd slept so late or so soundly.

Joe, of course, was no longer in her bed, but she knew he'd spent the night there. Even in her sleep, she'd been aware of his nearness.

She smiled to herself, a bittersweet smile that mirrored the feeling in her heart. How wonderful to be held as if she were loved. How sad not to be loved even while held.

But she refused to dwell on such thoughts. Not today. Like Scarlett O'Hara, she would think about it tomorrow. Or in her case, after her grandfather returned to Arizona and Joe moved out of the house for good.

Slowly—for it seemed she could do nothing in haste these days—she sat up, lowering her legs over the side of the bed. It was only as she started to rise to her feet that she realized the pain in her back was gone. Not so much as a tiny ache or twinge.

She could hardly wait to tell Joe what his back rub had accomplished. She wished she could also say what having him in her bed, holding her through the night, had done for her.

As it turned out, she wasn't able to tell him anything.

"He got a phone call while we were having breakfast," Grandpa Roger told her in the living room a short while later. "He said he'll be gone about an hour or two. And he wanted me to remind you to call your doctor."

"It's not necessary." She smiled, savoring her next words before she shared them. "Joe gave me a back rub last night, and it isn't bothering me at all this morning."

Joe gave me a back rub and then he held me in his arms and slept with me in my bed. And I love him with all my heart. I don't want him to leave me. I want him to remain with me forever and ever. How do I keep him with me, Grandpa? How do I make him love me?

"Well, I don't think that'll matter much to your husband," her grandfather responded. "He was adamant about you seeing your doctor today."

"I've got an appointment on Wednesday. That's soon enough."

"Young folk." He shook his head. "I guess you'll have to work that out between the two of you." He set aside the novel he'd been reading and rose from the easy chair. "Right now, let's get you some breakfast."

It was exactly the sort of apartment Joe'd had in mind for himself. Two bedrooms, one to sleep in and one he could use for an office when he worked late at home. Large windows and high ceilings that made it feel more spacious than it actually was. All the modern kitchen conveniences. A gas fireplace—no muss, no fuss. Reasonably quick access to downtown and the county courthouse. A view of the river from the living room; a view of the mountains from the master bedroom. A swimming pool, racquetball court, tennis court, workout room.

One problem, however—this was the only available unit and nothing was scheduled for vacancy in the next few months. If he wanted to live in this complex, he'd have to rent this apartment today. It would be gone by tomorrow.

He stared out the large window at the snow-bordered Boise River, frowning slightly.

It wasn't as if he couldn't afford to rent the place now and leave it empty for a couple of weeks. Besides, he could make arrangements for the movers to deliver his furniture between now and then. That way everything would be ready for him right on schedule.

He turned toward the rental manager. "I'll take it."

"Wonderful," Ms. Barton, an attractive woman in her early thirties, said with a smile. "Come to my office. Since you're a lawyer, I'm sure you know there's always plenty of paperwork to be seen to." The look she gave him was definitely what his mother would have called *come hither*.

Joe wasn't interested in coming hither, and he didn't bother to return her smile.

Once in the office he studied every word, every clause, of the lease before he signed it, but the memory of Alicia lying in his arms kept intruding, breaking his concentration. He was relieved when he could write the deposit and first month's rent check, hand it to Ms. Barton, and be on his way.

He told himself it was a minor miracle that he'd found an apartment at this time of the year. Nobody wanted to move over the holidays. It was an even greater miracle that he'd found a place with all the amenities he'd hoped for.

So why didn't he feel better about it?

That question played in his head over and over again as he drove toward home.

Home…

Therein lay the answer. The apartment he'd rented wasn't going to be home. Home was a drafty farmhouse with an attack cat who hissed at him and a mangy dog who stole things and chewed them to bits. Home had a Christmas tree decorated with homemade ornaments and a string of ancient bubble lights. Home had a kitchen with yellow walls, lace curtains at the windows, a Formica and chrome table, and ugly vinyl-covered chairs.

Home had all those things.

It also had Alicia.

Joe pulled his vehicle to the side of the road, then cut the engine. Silence filled the interior of his SUV.

Home, he realized, had nothing to do with the building or the things in it. Home from now on would be wherever Alicia was.

He didn't want to live in an apartment with all the modern conveniences. He didn't need a view of the river or the mountains, a swimming pool or a racquetball court. What he needed and wanted was exactly what he had.

What he needed and wanted was Alicia.

He gave his head a slow shake, marveling at the significance of his discovery. The miracle wasn't that he'd found an apartment to rent five days before Christmas.

The real miracle was that Joe had fallen in love with his wife.

Chapter Eighteen

The final few days before Christmas flew by.

Grandpa Roger had a friend take him out for some last-minute shopping. "Secrets are a part of the season," was the only explanation he would give Alicia.

Joe went to his interview and seemed pleased afterward. "I believe they'll ask me to join the firm," he told Alicia. "Looks like a good fit."

Alicia stayed busy, too, wrapping gifts, baking cookies and beginning to put the nursery in order after the wallpapering was finished. But her small world seemed off-kilter somehow, though she couldn't say precisely how or why. Perhaps it was because she longed to ask Joe to return to her bed but lacked the courage to do so. Or perhaps it was the way he watched her whenever they were together, as if she were a puzzle to be solved.

On Christmas Eve, Grandpa Roger, Alicia and Joe attended the candlelight service at church. It was another special memory for her to treasure in her heart. Perhaps all the more so because she realized how soon both Joe and her grandfather would be leaving, how few memories she still had time to gather.

Upon their return home, Alicia filled large Santa mugs with hot chocolate, and the three of them sat in the living room, watching the bubble lights and sipping their beverages. For a time each was lost in private thoughts.

It was Grandpa Roger who broke the silence. "What about the baby's name? Have you two come to an agreement yet?"

"Not yet," Alicia answered.

"You're running out of time, you know."

"We know."

She hated the lies. They seemed to pile up at an alarming rate. And lying to her grandfather on Christmas Eve seemed worse than usual. But the die had been cast weeks ago. She had no choice except to say the things he expected to hear.

"We just haven't found the perfect names, Grandpa. That's all."

"And what about you, Joe?" the old man asked. "Any favorites yet?"

"Well, sir, the truth is, I've grown rather fond of Humphrey." Joe winked at Alicia.

Both his words and his teasing wink took her by surprise. She didn't know how to respond to either.

"Hmm." Grandpa Roger set his mug on the coffee table. "It's time to remind you that I won't be present when my great-grandchild is born. I'd like to make certain he or she isn't named in haste." He frowned at Joe. "Humphrey Palermo, indeed."

"I suppose you're right," Joe answered, drawing out his words, as if giving them serious consideration. Then he said, "Actually, sir, I was thinking more along the lines of Teresa if it's a girl." He met Alicia's gaze. "After the baby's Great-Grandmother Harris."

Her eyes flooded with tears.

"That would have pleased my wife," Grandpa Roger said. "It pleases me, as well. Thank you from the bottom of an old man's heart." He paused, cleared his throat, then asked, "And if it's a boy?"

Even though she couldn't see him clearly, she knew Joe continued to watch her.

"The Palermos always give their firstborn sons the name Enrico, either as a first or middle name. It's a tradition I'd like to keep."

Determined not to burst into tears, she managed to say, "Your name isn't Enrico."

"I wasn't the first son. My older brother was stillborn. He was named Enrico."

Did her grandfather wonder why she didn't know that?

Joe covered for her. "Guess I should have told you before now." He shrugged. "Losing him wasn't something my family talked about. I guess it became a habit not to."

She looked down at her belly. "We could call him Ricky," she said in a whisper.

"I like that." Joe took hold of her hand. "Ricky Palermo it is."

*　*　*

Joe was waiting for them to be alone so he could tell Alicia he loved her, to tell her he didn't want to be her husband for the holidays. He wanted to be her husband for the rest of his life. He wanted her baby to be their baby, to be a Palermo, to have however many brothers and sisters might follow.

He couldn't have explained why he didn't speak up the instant her grandfather retired for the night, but he didn't.

Call it nerves.

Call it habit.

Call it stupidity.

Whatever the reason, he didn't tell her, and because of it he spent another long, sleepless night on that danged sofa bed.

At the opposite side of the bedroom Alicia lay awake, as well, replaying the evening in her mind and hoping against hope it meant what she wanted it to mean. It was possible Joe had been merely playing the role expected of him. He'd become adept at it over the weeks.

And yet...

Ricky Palermo.

The baby moved within her womb, as if recognizing his name. She laid both hands on her belly.

Is it possible? Could it be true? Oh, please. Let it be true.

Alicia paused in the living room, arrested by the view.

Joe stood in the bright-yellow kitchen, leaning his behind against the counter, his legs angled before him, right ankle crossed over left. He wore jeans and a sweatshirt, but his feet were bare, as if he thought it summer, not winter. In his right hand, he held a coffee mug, and he sipped from it, his eyes closed.

He looked…contented.

Oh, how she longed for that to be true. She loved him. She wanted him. She needed him. If only he could love, want and need her, too.

Is it possible?

As if she'd spoken aloud, he opened his eyes and glanced her way. His smile was slow and sleepy. "Merry Christmas."

Her heart leaped in response. Could it be true?

"Merry Christmas, Joe."

"Did you peek under the tree?"

Oh, please. Let it be true.

"No."

"I'd've thought you the type to do that."

She returned his smile. "I am."

"Want some breakfast while we wait for Grandpa to wake up?"

She nodded. Please let it be true.

"You set the table," he said, "and I'll scramble the eggs."

"Deal."

After setting down his coffee mug, he strode across the kitchen to the refrigerator. He was bent forward, looking inside the appliance, when Rosie jumped through the pet door, almost onto his foot. She slid to a halt, paws scrambling on the slick linoleum. Her back arched as high as it could go, and she hissed at him.

"Cat—" he pointed an index finger at the animal

"—you and I are gonna come to terms before we're through."

Rosie growled but didn't move.

"Ask Rags. She'll tell you I'm one of the good guys."

Happiness flooded through Alicia as she watched and listened. It was useless to deny what she felt, what she wanted, what she hoped for.

Joe reached out, as if to pet the cat's head. Rosie took a swipe at his hand, barely missing her target. Then she darted out of the kitchen.

He straightened and looked at Alicia. "I'm not crying uncle yet. I'm determined she'll get used to me."

I love you, Joe. Can you see it in my eyes?

He stared at her, the look intense and unwavering; his smile faded.

Can you hear it calling from my heart?

"Alicia..."

Her pulse quickened.

"There's something I need to—" The sound of a closing door intruded on his words. He stopped and glanced toward the living room.

A few moments later Grandpa Roger appeared. "Merry Christmas," he said with a cheerful grin, his gaze moving from Alicia to Joe and then back again.

"Merry Christmas, Grandpa."

"Merry Christmas, sir."

"Hope you haven't been waiting long."

"No, sir. We haven't."

Alicia wondered what Joe might have said if her grandfather had waited a little while longer.

Even though Grandpa Roger's arrival had been untimely, interrupting Joe's declaration of love, Joe wasn't discouraged. A sixth sense told him he would find the right moment, an even better moment, to tell Alicia what he had to say. That same intuition told him he needn't fear her response. She loved him, too.

The future looked better than he'd imagined it could.

And this was the best of all Christmases, too. When Joe was growing up, this time of the year had been about getting the latest gizmo. It had been about giving the gift with the most prestige or the biggest price tag.

But that wasn't what it was about in Alicia's home. It was about caring. He'd already witnessed that truth in the weeks he'd been here, but it became crystal clear when he opened Alicia's final gift to him.

In the box was a black leather day planner with his name etched on a gold plate in the lower right corner. The binder was nicer than the one he'd lost, but it was what he found inside the covers of the planner that truly touched his heart. By some miracle, Alicia had duplicated most of the pages Rags destroyed, the ones Joe had given up for lost. Pages upon pages, including his extensive address book, were filled with her meticulous, legible handwriting.

"When did you find time to do this?"

"Here and there," she answered with a gentle smile.

Joe tried to think of something to say to express what he felt. Words eluded him. The best he could manage was a simple "Thanks." He stood. "Now I've got something more for you. Sit tight."

He felt as excited as a kid in a candy store as he

hurried out of the living room, into the kitchen and down the basement stairs. He knew Alicia was going to be surprised.

Satisfaction warmed Roger Harris.

If he'd had any doubts that Alicia and Joe belonged together—which he hadn't had—those doubts would have been assuaged this morning. Watching the two of them was like looking into the face of love itself. Whatever problems had plagued them a couple of weeks earlier seemed to have been overcome.

Roger was thankful for that.

He stared at the brightly lit tree with its dancing bubble lights, and his thoughts drifted back in time. He recalled the many Christmas mornings he and his beloved Teresa had shared. They'd had a good marriage, a blessed life. Of course, they'd had their share of heartaches and disappointments; no marriage ever escaped the bad times completely. The rain fell on the just and the unjust. But love had seen them through, seen them through and brought them closer together.

He lifted a silent prayer, asking God to grant many years, many *good* years, to his granddaughter and her husband. He prayed their love would sustain them no matter what tomorrow might bring.

Love always sustained.

Alicia shifted her position on the sofa, seeking a physical comfort that would not be found. The ache in her back had returned. If not for Joe and her grandfather, she'd have gone back to bed. But they would worry if she did, and the day was too perfect to allow that. Besides, she could hardly bear the suspense, waiting to see what had caused Joe to look so excited, so pleased with himself as he'd hurried from the room.

She heard him climbing the stairs and she turned expectantly toward the kitchen doorway.

Before he came into view, he called out, "Close your eyes, Alicia."

"Joe—" she began in protest.

"Close 'em."

She released a dramatic sigh. "All right." She obeyed.

"Are they closed, sir?"

"They are, indeed," her grandfather replied.

Alicia folded her hands atop her abdomen, clenching them tightly while resisting the urge to peek. She heard Joe's footsteps on the hardwood floor, knew the moment he reached the sofa. She worried her lower lip between her teeth.

"Don't look yet."

She smiled. "You're enjoying this *way* too much, Joe Palermo."

"Uh-huh."

"Rat."

"Uh-huh."

She heard him set something on the floor.

"I got a call from Susie a while back."

"Susie?" Why was he talking about her assistant manager? And why would Susie call him?

"The supplier for that cradle you had your heart set on can't deliver one until spring."

Broadsided by the disappointing news, she forgot to keep her eyes closed. Her mouth was already open to ask why he hadn't told her about the call...

And then she saw the wooden cradle set before her. She looked from it to Joe and back again.

"I had it made," he said, answering her unspoken question. "I hope it's close enough to what you wanted."

"You had it made?" She slipped from the sofa and onto her knees, touching the smooth wood of the cradle, causing it to swing gently.

"A local guy. He came highly recommended. A real artisan. I think he did a good job, even if he did have to work fast."

"It's beautiful. It's wonderful." She looked up. "How can I ever thank you for this?"

Joe knelt on the opposite side of the cradle. "You don't have to thank me," he answered softly, debating whether or not to lean forward and kiss her.

He needed to be alone with her. He needed to tell her that he loved her and wanted to be her husband forever. He needed to tell her all the things he'd discovered since coming to stay with her. He'd waited long enough.

"Why don't we put this in the nursery now?" he suggested.

She smiled. "Okay." Her response was tremulous, a telltale quiver in her lower lip that warned she was fighting tears.

Joe stood, then took both her hands in his and helped her do the same. He squeezed her fingers gently, reluctant to release his hold on her.

I'm not ever going to let go of you, Alicia. Not in any of the ways that count. I'm going to stay with you and love you for the rest of my life.

He squeezed her fingers a second time, feeling a

bit misty-eyed himself. Then he reached for the cradle. "Lead the way."

She was almost to the hall when she stopped and looked back at him. "I've got a bumper and matching baby blanket down in the basement. I'm going to get them. I want to see how it all looks."

She hurried away before he could stop her.

He sighed. He supposed he could wait.

After all, what difference could a few minutes make in comparison to a lifetime?

Chapter Nineteen

Rags had been up to her old tricks again.

"What am I going to do with you?" Alicia muttered as she bent to retrieve the legal-size document with the canine teeth marks clearly stamped upon it.

She was already walking toward Joe's office, meaning to leave the papers on his desk, when the words *Lease Agreement* penetrated her mind. She stopped still; her breath caught in her throat. With unbelieving eyes, she scanned the front page, then turned to the second.

Joseph Palermo was scrawled on the signature line. The contract was dated December 20.

Five days ago.

On Sunday he'd rubbed her back, then stayed in her bed, holding her throughout the night.

On Monday he'd signed a lease for his new apartment.

She'd known all along he intended to move after her grandfather returned to Arizona. This shouldn't have caught her by surprise, and yet it had. Because she'd started to believe he loved her.

But he didn't love her. He couldn't love her. He'd told her so several times, yet she'd chosen to ignore the truth. She couldn't do that any longer. She mustn't.

For his sake as well as for her own.

"Hey, you coming?" Joe called down to her.

"Yes." Still holding the lease agreement in one hand, she grabbed the bumper pad and blanket and cradle sheet, then walked toward the stairs. "I'm coming."

He was waiting for her in the kitchen. "I set the cradle near the window," he said as he cupped her left elbow with one of his hands. "But I think I can feel a draft through the glass."

He was a good, kind man, she thought, allowing him to propel her toward the nursery. He'd done her an enormous favor, even going so far as to marry her for the sake of her grandfather's health. It wasn't his fault he couldn't love her. She had no right to feel hurt and betrayed.

"So?" He released her arm and stepped ahead of her into the room. "What do you think?"

"Joe, I—"

The telephone rang. She ignored it.

"I think we need to talk," she finished softly, closing the nursery door behind her.

Joe smiled, a look that first melted her heart, then broke it in two. "Yes, we do need to talk."

"About this." She dropped the items in her arms,

then held the lease papers toward him. "Rags got into your office again."

He took the lease from her, glanced at it, looked at her again. He wasn't smiling now. "I didn't mean for you to see this."

"Why? Didn't you want me to know where you were going to live?"

"No." He stepped closer. "You misunderstood. I didn't—"

The nursery door opened behind her.

"Excuse me," her grandfather said. "Alicia, you're wanted on the phone."

"Not now, Grandpa."

"I think this could be important." His voice was grave. "The man claims to be your ex-husband and the father of your baby. I believe he said his name is Grant."

Joe scowled. "I'll handle this."

"No." She grabbed his arm. "It's my problem. Not yours."

"Alicia, you—"

She turned toward her grandfather. "It's time we all faced the truth. Joe isn't the father of my baby. He's my husband in name only, and as soon as you return to Arizona, he's moving out and getting a divorce." She glanced over her shoulder, her gaze colliding with Joe's. "Maybe you shouldn't wait to move. There's no reason for you to, now that Grandpa knows."

Woodenly, she walked to the kitchen to take Grant's unwelcome call.

Joe stared after her, not knowing what to do next.

He needed to explain that he'd changed his mind, that he loved her, that she'd misunderstood everything.

"Is it true?" Grandpa Roger asked.

Joe looked at the older man. "Yes."

"Why? I'm afraid I don't understand."

"She didn't want to worry you. She married Grant against your advice, then ended up divorced and pregnant. She wanted to tell you, but she was afraid your heart couldn't take the truth."

Grandpa Roger sank onto the rocking chair. "God forgive me," he whispered, lowering his gaze to the floor.

"We meant well, sir." What a pitiful excuse for deception.

Silence held the room in an icy grip, stretching from one minute to two, from two minutes to three, from three minutes to four. To Joe it seemed more like an eternity. He didn't know whether to be relieved or dismayed when Alicia returned.

She paused inside the doorway. Both men looked at her. The air was heavy with anticipation and dread.

"Grant wanted to make certain he wasn't going to have a tax problem," she said at last, answering their unspoken questions. "I assured him he wouldn't."

"Taxes?" Joe repeated, incredulous. "On Christmas morning?"

Her smile was devoid of humor. "You'd have to know Grant to understand."

Joe clenched his hands into fists. He didn't want to know Grant Reeves. But if they ever met, Joe would do his best to knock some sense into him.

Grandpa Roger rose to his feet. "I'd like to hear the whole story, Alicia."

"Yes. You deserve an explanation." Her gaze shifted from him to Joe. "But we can do that after you leave."

"Wait a minute. Alicia, I don't—"

"No," she interrupted. "It's time, Joe. It isn't fair to either of us to drag this out. You've been a good sport to help me the way you have. You came to Idaho to ski and enjoy yourself and practice law with a new firm, but all you've done is take care of me and pretend to be something you're not. You've gone way beyond what I should've asked of you. You've been unfailingly kind, a dear, dear friend, and I'll always be grateful. But it's time for you to go. You've rented your apartment. If you need some furnishings or dishes or anything else to get you temporarily by, you can take what you want and return it when your own things arrive from wherever."

"But what about—"

"Don't." She raised a hand to stop his protest. "Please don't argue with me. You know I'm right. You've never pretended it would last longer than necessary." Her voice was flat and emotionless. There were no signs of tears now. "And it's no longer necessary. Just pack up and go. You can file the papers on Monday to start the divorce. You'll have no problems from me. It will happen just as we agreed."

She stared at him a moment longer, as if searching for something.

Apparently she failed to find it.

She turned and left the nursery.

As soon as they were alone, Joe faced her grandfather. "Sir, this isn't what I wanted."

"No, son," the old man said softly, "I don't imagine it is. But it's what you got.'' He walked toward the door, then paused and said, ''I think you'd better do as she asked. Your presence doesn't seem to be required.''

Shoulders slumped and his footsteps heavy, Grandpa Roger walked away, leaving Joe completely to himself.

Alicia took refuge in the guest room. It was the only room Joe wouldn't need to enter as he gathered his things to leave. She stood at the window, staring out at the winter snowscape, wondering why it didn't look as lovely as it had an hour before.

''Here you are,'' her grandfather said from behind her.

She heard the door close. A few moments later her grandfather's hand alighted on her right shoulder. She tilted her head toward it, communicating without words how much it meant to have him with her.

''I plan to stay,'' he said. ''As long as you want me with you, I'll stay.''

''Oh, Grandpa. I don't need to upset your life. Your home is in Arizona. You've loved it there. All your friends are there.''

''And all my family is here.''

She'd thought herself too numb to cry. She'd been wrong. The tears came, slipping down her cheeks in silent testimony to the brokenness of her heart.

''Come here,'' her grandfather gently commanded. ''Sit beside me on the bed, and we'll talk.''

She didn't want to talk. She wanted to hide. She wanted to crawl into bed, pull the covers over her head and hide there forever.

Such was not her fate.

Seated next to her grandfather, responding to his carefully posed questions, Alicia told him every-thing—about her hasty marriage and her equally hasty divorce, about her fears after his heart attack, about her chat room encounter with Joe, even about the pre-nuptial agreement she'd signed before she and Joe entered into their pretense of a marriage. Grandpa Roger held her hand as she spoke, nodding occasion-ally but revealing no other reaction.

When the full truth had been disclosed, Alicia sighed and closed her eyes, awaiting her grandfather's judgment. She would deserve it, no matter what it was.

"This is partially my fault," he said.

That wasn't what she'd expected. She looked at him in confusion.

He nodded. "I never should have forced you to marry. I should have known there were sound reasons for your decision. I should have trusted you more."

"But you had no way of—"

"And I shouldn't have lied to keep you together." He shook his head.

"Lied?"

He sighed. "Yes. I knew things weren't right. I overheard you talking in the nursery. The day Joe was wallpapering. I heard him say he wasn't good hus-band material, and I heard you say the marriage couldn't work." He shook his head again. "I was so certain you loved each other. I thought if you had enough time, you could work it out. So I returned to the kitchen, slammed the back door and faked not feeling well. I thought I'd done the right thing for you both.''

''You weren't completely wrong, Grandpa.'' She placed an arm around his back. ''I do love Joe.''

He met her gaze. ''Then why are you sending him away?''

''Because he doesn't love me.''

He opened his mouth as if to argue with her, then closed it again, apparently deciding silence was the better response.

Joe packed his possessions in his SUV. He didn't borrow any furnishings or kitchen items. He didn't want to have to return them. He could get by for one night. Tomorrow morning the stores would open for their after-Christmas sales. He could stock up then.

When he was ready to go, the small bag of bathroom toiletries in his hand, he stopped in the hall and looked toward the guest room door. It remained closed. He wondered if he should knock and say goodbye.

No, he answered himself. Alicia wouldn't want him to do that. She just wanted him gone.

It was for the best. He'd told her from the start this deception was a mistake. He'd also told her he didn't want to be a husband or a father. He'd suffered a momentary lapse in judgment, thinking otherwise for a few days, but he'd been rescued from making a tragic mistake by the odd events of this morning.

He'd been so close to telling her he loved her.

He'd been so close to telling her he wanted her baby to be his.

Undeniably, certifiably insane.

He paused long enough in the kitchen to remove her house key from his key ring. He left it on the counter near the coffeepot.

It didn't take him long to drive to his Boise apartment. The streets were mostly deserted on Christmas Day. After all, people with families were with them.

Joe had no one.

The lease for his new residence had required the utilities be transferred to his name upon signing, so at least he wouldn't be without heat and lights until Monday. That was a blessing, he told himself. He even had an activated phone jack. Of course, he didn't have a phone to plug into it, but he could pick one up tomorrow as soon as the stores opened. Until then, he had his cell phone if the need arose.

Three trips between vehicle and apartment, and he'd moved in.

While the furnace pumped heat into the chilled rooms, Joe set his stereo to a station playing pop music—anything other than sounds of the holiday—then he flicked on the gas fireplace for ambience.

Neither served to improve his sense of isolation.

He thought of Alicia. He thought of the things he might have said, the things he might have done. He thought of what might have been.

But he didn't want to think. He didn't want to feel.

He got out his laptop, determined to work for the remainder of the day. He needed to start acting like the driven attorney he'd always been.

Alicia was standing at the kitchen counter, holding the house key Joe had left behind, when her water broke. She gasped in surprise, uncertain at first what was happening. Then a band of pain tightened around her abdomen. It wasn't particularly strong nor was it unbearable, but it was definitely pain.

"Grandpa, come quick!"

The key clattered to the floor as another rush of fluid was discharged.

"Grandpa!" she cried, gripping the counter with both hands.

"What is it?"

"My water broke." She looked at her grandfather as he entered the kitchen. "It's too soon. The baby isn't due for three weeks."

"Stay calm. Babies are known to set their own timetables." He patted her shoulder and gave her an encouraging smile, then he walked toward the telephone. "Where's your doctor's number?"

"On the bulletin board. Dr. Jamison." She pointed, grimacing as the pain strengthened. "In the upper right-hand corner. That's his business card."

"I'll call him. You go get your things together. We'll leave for the hospital as soon as we can get a cab."

The pain was lessening. "I could drive."

"Nonsense." Grandpa Roger lifted the receiver, then hesitated with his index finger poised above the keys. He glanced over his shoulder. "Go on. Get your suitcase."

As she headed toward her bedroom, she prayed silently for her baby to be all right.

Her small suitcase had been packed for a couple of weeks now. Actually, it had been packed and unpacked at least twice a week for the past two months. It sat on the floor right next to the door. She thought about opening it, maybe taking some things out, putting something else in. She was stopped by another pain spreading from the small of her back and wrapping around her belly.

"Please don't let anything go wrong," she whispered. She braced her abdomen between her hands. "We're going to be happy, you and I. I promise. I'll make you a good mother, Ricky."

Tears sprang to her eyes.

Humphrey, she reminded herself. Not Ricky Palermo. Humphrey Harris.

The pain receded once again. Alicia took a deep breath, then picked up her suitcase and started toward the kitchen. She stopped outside the nursery. Her gaze rested on the cradle. Inside it was the stuffed toy seal Joe had purchased at Bundles of Joy the day after he'd arrived in Idaho. She didn't know when he'd put it there. Probably while he was packing to leave.

She entered the nursery, crossed to the cradle and picked up the stuffed animal with her free hand. She pressed the toy to her chest, remembering the day Joe had bought it. She wished...

But it was useless to wish for things she couldn't have.

She walked out of the nursery, still clutching the toy.

Despite all of Joe's best efforts, he accomplished nothing. His thoughts drifted again and again to Alicia. To Alicia and her grandfather and her baby. To the fact that he loved her and didn't want to lose her.

He'd made plenty of mistakes. It was his own fault she'd asked him to leave. He shouldn't have waited to tell her what he'd discovered. But that didn't mean his mistakes couldn't be undone.

Only an idiot would let her go.

Only an idiot would give her up without a fight.

And Joe Palermo was no idiot.

He grabbed his car keys and his coat and headed for the door.

Chapter Twenty

"It's too early," Alicia told the nurse, just as she'd told everyone at the hospital. "I'm not due for three more weeks."

Nurse Beverly reassured her with a pat on the hand. "The fetal heartbeat is strong, and there are no signs of trouble. My guess is you've got a fully developed baby in there who's eager to meet the world."

"But—"

"Stop worrying, Ms. Harris. You're going to have enough to do in the next few hours."

"When will Dr. Jamison be in to see me?"

The nurse smiled patiently. "When he's finished his Christmas dinner, I imagine."

"He isn't on his way *now?*" Alicia's voice rose a notch with each word.

"You've got a ways to go, dear. Try to relax as

much as you can. Take a walk around the halls. That sometimes speeds the process. And don't worry. The doctor will get here in plenty of time.''

Alicia would have sworn Nurse Beverly was chuckling softly as she left the birthing room.

A few minutes later Grandpa Roger appeared in the doorway. "Am I allowed in yet?''

"Yes. Come in.''

"What news?'' Her grandfather approached the bed.

"I'm supposed to relax and enjoy myself.'' She sounded petulant, even in her own ears.

Grandpa Roger grinned.

She scooted off the table, feeling awkward, hating the hospital-issued gown. "If you laugh, Grandpa, I'll strangle you. I swear I will.''

He nearly choked on it, but he managed to heed her warning.

"Come on. Let's walk.'' She put on her robe, then hooked her arm through his. Once they were out in the hall, she asked, "Did you call Susie?''

"Yes, but I got her answering machine.''

"Feel up to being my coach?''

He patted her arm. "The old man is honored to be asked.'' He chuckled softly. "Don't know how much help I'll be. In my day men were relegated to the waiting room.''

She thought of Joe and the birthing classes. She remembered how she'd leaned against his chest, the way he'd touched her abdomen, the deep timbre of his voice.

I need you, Joe. I want you with me.

* * *

When nobody answered the door after several rings, Joe began to worry. Alicia's car was in the garage, but the house appeared to be empty. No sounds came from within. It was possible she'd seen who was outside and was ignoring him. If that was the case, he should leave.

But he couldn't shake the feeling something was wrong. He used the key Alicia kept hidden beneath a stone near the back porch.

"Alicia?"

He stepped into the kitchen.

"Mr. Harris?"

Rags galloped into the kitchen, acting delighted to see him.

"Hello, girl." He patted the dog's head. "Where's your mistress? Where's Alicia?"

The back of his neck tingled as he walked through the empty house, Rags following at his heels. He searched all the rooms on the main floor, then he checked the basement, then he checked the main floor a second time. He told himself not to panic, but it was getting harder to listen to the voice of reason.

He considered calling the police, but there was no sign of foul play. And they just might arrest him for breaking and entering.

Perhaps Alicia and Grandpa Roger had gone somewhere with a friend. Maybe they went with Susie to a movie. It hadn't been an exactly joyous Christmas Day in the Harris household. Maybe Alicia had wanted to take her mind off him…most likely with a senselessly violent movie.

When he entered the master bedroom for the third time, he was greeted by Rosie's familiar growl. The feline was coiled on the sofa bed, watching him with a haughty glare.

"I don't have time to mess with you, cat."

He turned to leave and then stopped.

The suitcase. Alicia's maternity suitcase. She'd kept it by the door, and now it was gone.

His pulse quickened with alarm. The "don't panic" command was useless now. He raced to the kitchen where he yanked the phone directory from its drawer. With clumsy fingers he leafed through the pages until he found the listing for the hospital. In the midst of dialing the number, he had to hang up twice due to punching the wrong keys. But finally he did it right.

He barely let the receptionist say the hospital's name before he was asking, "Has an Alicia Harris checked into the maternity ward?"

He assumed the following silence meant the woman was checking her records.

"Yes, sir. She's there now."

"Thanks," he said a split second before dropping the receiver in its cradle.

He was out at his vehicle in a flash.

Mothers in labor walked the halls of the maternity ward, going around and around and around the same circuitous route. Occasionally one of them would change directions, simply to break the monotony. When they passed one another, they smiled, as if their conditions had made them friends, comrades in arms.

Alicia's pains had grown steadily in intensity, and yet the nurse said she had a long ways to go before serious labor would begin. Little Humphrey Harris,

Alicia decided around her third hour of labor, was going to be an only child.

At five o'clock, she insisted Grandpa Roger go to the cafeteria for supper.

When he tried to argue with her, she snapped, "You'll do me no good if you make yourself sick. Now please go and eat something."

She was ashamed of her tone, but there was no taking the words back.

After her grandfather left the room, Alicia sat on the window ledge and stared at the darkening sky.

I wonder how close I am to Joe's apartment.

She'd recognized the address on the lease. She knew the upscale complex was near the Boise River. If the hospital had more floors... If the ancient oaks and elms didn't rise so tall above the stately homes... If—

"But she's my wife!"

Alicia turned as the door to her room burst open and Joe pushed his way past the nurse.

"I'm sorry, Ms. Harris," the flustered young woman said. "I'll call security."

She rose to her feet, pulling her robe more closely around her. "No. It's all right."

The nurse didn't look convinced.

Joe took another step into the room. "Tell her I'm your husband."

"We're married." That was somehow more honest than what he'd asked her to say.

"I came as soon as I found out," he said.

"How did you know?"

He glanced at the nurse, his gaze demanding she leave them alone.

"It's all right," Alicia said again. "Really."

Joe waited until the door swung closed before saying, "I went back to the house. It was empty. Your suitcase was gone."

"Oh."

"Do you want to know why?"

"Why what?"

"Why I went back to the house."

She crossed her arms over her chest. "I assume you left something behind."

"Yes. As a matter of fact, I did." He took another step forward. "You."

"Oh, Joe." She turned toward the window, watching as the city came alive with lights. "You don't have to pretend any longer."

"I'm not pretending. This is for real. This is the most real I've been in my life. I love you, Alicia."

Another pain crept around her abdomen, making it difficult to think, difficult to breathe. She did her best not to let on.

"I want to be your husband in every definition of the word."

Sheer resolve kept her voice steady. "You don't want kids, and in case you haven't noticed...I do. And very soon, too."

"I was wrong."

"Were you?" She faced him again. "I think you stated your feelings quite clearly in your daddy clause."

He frowned. "My daddy clause?"

"In the prenuptial." She was *not* going to cry. She was *not* going to cry. "About my baby."

"Oh. That."

The urge to cry vanished, driven away by anger. "Yes, *that!* *This* is the baby you didn't want." She pressed her hands against the sides of her abdomen. "*This* is the baby you wanted to make certain no one thought was yours. *This* was—"

Her words were cut short by a sharp, searing pain. She gasped, and her knees buckled. Joe caught her in his arms before she could fall.

"What is it?"

"I think it's time," she managed to say through gritted teeth. "Help me to the bed and then call the nurse."

Things happened quickly after that.

The attractive birthing room with its soft lights, muted wallpaper and homey furnishings changed in an instant to the epitome of modern medical technology. Bright overhead lights swung out of a closet, slipping into position above the bed. All the necessary hospital equipment and paraphernalia appeared from different nooks and cubbyholes, as if by magic. Nurses bustled about doing nurse-type things.

Joe was in the way. He figured most men were at a time like this. As a matter of fact, he would have liked to be anywhere else in the world rather than here. He felt useless, and that wasn't a feeling he was used to or comfortable with.

But it would take more than discomfort to drive him out now.

He stepped to the side of Alicia's bed. "I'll write you a new daddy clause."

She gave him a sharp look.

"Every firstborn Palermo male is named Enrico. We need to get that settled before he gets here."

She clenched her jaw, and a groan came up from deep in her chest.

Joe looked at a nurse. "Is she all right?"

"She's about to have a baby," came the terse reply.

"Where can I get pen and paper?"

"Try the desk," the nurse answered. He was walking toward the door when he heard her add, "Men. Anything to keep them out of the way."

"I'll be right back, Alicia."

He yanked open the door...and there stood Roger Harris. The elderly man didn't seem surprised to see him.

"Evening, sir."

"Evening, Joe."

"Will you marry us before our baby arrives?"

Alicia's grandfather raised an eyebrow. "You are married."

"Just legally, sir. This would be different. I love her. I want her to know that."

Grandpa Roger smiled. "I'll do it if that's what Alicia wants."

"She's going to want it." He took off down the hall toward the nurse's station.

Breathing hard from the most recent contraction, Alicia asked the nurse, "Where's the doctor?"

"He's on his way. He'll be here soon."

The door opened. Alicia thought it would be the doctor. It wasn't.

Joe strode across the spacious room, legal pad in hand. Alicia's grandfather was right behind him.

She leaned back on the pillow. "I don't think you should be in here."

"I'm your birth coach. Remember? I *do* belong here." He held out the paper, covered with his bold penmanship. "Read this."

"Are you crazy?" She sounded as irritable as she felt. "In case you can't tell, I'm *busy* at the moment."

He grinned.

She considered homicide.

"Okay, I'll do it." He leaned close, and in a soft voice began to read. "I, Joseph Palermo, do solemnly swear that I will love, cherish and honor my wife, Alicia Harris Palermo, for the rest of my life."

The bright overhead lights seemed to recede. All she could see was Joe's beloved face. All she could hear was his beloved voice.

"I will be faithful and true and will never hurt her intentionally. I will provide for her welfare and support her pursuit of her own dreams, whatever they may be. I further declare that I will be a loving father to our child, born this Christmas Day, and I will raise him or her, in partnership with my wife, to the best of my abilities. Should God bless us with more children in the years to come, I will do the same for them."

Alicia wondered if this was the strangest delivery room scene these nurses had ever witnessed.

"And finally, should there be any question, I promise to love the dogs who chew up my important papers and the cats who take chunks out of my hide. I'll love them because they are hers."

She couldn't see him any longer. Her eyes were swimming in tears. And if she wasn't mistaken, at least one of the nurses was sniffling.

Joe took her hand. "I love you. I don't want to be your holiday husband. I want to be your husband for a lifetime. Humphrey is our baby. You know it as much as I do. I want your grandfather to marry us again. For real this time. Let me play Santa Claus for our kids as they grow up. Let me chop down all your Christmas trees. Let me drink your spiced cider while we watch the bubble lights bubble. Marry me, Alicia. Say yes."

She would have answered, if not for the contraction that suddenly gripped her. She groaned and gritted her teeth.

"I think that's a yes, sir. Time to say the appropriate words. And I think you'd better hurry, too."

Epilogue

Alicia knew her husband had been watching her sleep. It was something he did often. She smiled, warmed by the knowledge and feeling wonderfully content because of it.

"Good morning, sleepyhead," Joe whispered.

She opened her eyes slowly. He lay on his side, his elbow propped on the pillow, his head braced on the heel of his hand. Pale morning sunlight filtered through the window blinds, allowing her to see the loving expression in his eyes.

"Good morning," she murmured.

He leaned forward and kissed her—one of those slow, long kisses that caused heat to race through her veins and her heart to palpitate. A kiss that held a wonderful promise of all that could follow, a promise that had been fulfilled during the night just past.

"Ricky's still asleep," he said when their lips parted.

She smiled again, this time a smile of knowing invitation.

"Temptress."

"Uh-huh."

Joe laid the palm of his hand on her cheek, then traced a slow path down her throat, over her collarbone and finally to its resting place on her breast. The intimate touch caused another surge of heat to coil through her.

She wondered if their six-week-old infant would sleep long enough for his father to make love to his mother.

Ricky's first whimpering complaint answered her silent question.

Joe chuckled softly. "Little tyrant." He kissed her again, then said, "Stay here. I'll get him."

It was one of those simple things in life that Alicia took great pleasure in, watching him be the daddy he hadn't thought he wanted to be.

Clad in the shorts and T-shirt he wore for pajamas, Joe rose and walked to the cradle. He leaned over the baby's bed, speaking softly in words Alicia couldn't quite make out. In short order he changed Ricky's diaper, as if he'd done it a thousand times.

Cat's paws made pattering sounds across the floor, announcing Rosie's arrival. A moment later, she began to purr.

"Not now, Rosie," Joe said gently.

Although Alicia couldn't see what was happening, she knew the cat was winding her way around his ankles, her tail carried high as she demanded his affections. The change in the feline's attitude toward Joe was just one more in a long list of small miracles that made up Alicia's life these days.

Joe lifted their son from the cradle and returned to the bed where he lay on his back, holding the baby on his chest. Ricky fussed a moment or two longer, then fell back to sleep.

"Guess he wasn't ready for breakfast yet," Joe whispered. He held out his free arm. "Come here and join us."

Alicia was only too happy to oblige. She slid across the mattress, drawing close against his side, her cheek resting on his shoulder.

"Better sleep while you can," he suggested softly.

"I know."

But she didn't close her eyes. She wanted to look at the two of them a little longer, father and son, Joseph and Ricky Palermo, SkiBum and his future MogulMonster.

"What're you grinning about?" he asked, amused suspicion in his voice.

"Everything, Joe," she whispered. "Absolutely everything."

*   *   *   *   *

Silhouette Stars

Born this Month

Monica Seles, Walt Disney, Jeff Bridges, James Galway, Frank Sinatra, Lee Remick, Keith Richards, Jenny Agutter, Uri Geller, Mary Tyler Moore

Star of the Month

Sagittarius

A year of progress in many areas of your life, however, effort will be needed to organise yourself properly in order to make the best of what is on offer. Romance is well aspected and you could find yourself making a commitment early next year. Take care over finances, read all the small print before signing contracts.

SILH/HR/0012a

Capricorn

A career move is on the cards but you will need to decide if it is what you want. It could be worth all the disruption that it might cause to your life.

Aquarius

A happy go lucky month with lots of social events on offer. Forget your troubles and catch up on old friends and with opportunities to make new ones too, you should have a ball!

 Pisces

There is the promise of a brighter, happier period in which you may achieve something that's been top of your wish-list for a long while. You could surprise a lot of people, not least yourself!

Aries

The focus is on the home where you will find real happiness and contentment. Old friends make contact and you may be planning an 'out of the ordinary' holiday together.

 Taurus

A busy month with plenty to be done around the home. Enlist the help of those around to make the job quicker and allow you time to relax as well. A touching surprise from a loved one could really lift your spirits.

Gemini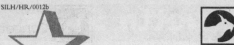

There should be good reason to celebrate this month as the dark clouds lift and you see your life progressing positively. One particular gift brings a wry smile to your face.

SILH/HR/0012c

  Cancer

Listen to your inner soul and act on what you really feel as it could save you from making a big mistake. An old friend re-enters your life late in the month.

Leo

A new opportunity to study, re-train or work in an area that suits you should not be missed. A loved one could pleasantly surprise you mid-month.

 Virgo

A great time to start a new project as you should be feeling very creative. A romantic encounter sets your pulse racing, but take care, all may not be as it seems.

Libra

Wipe away the winter blues, take up a new activity, revamp the home. By keeping busy you will feel more positive and your energy will create opportunity.

 Scorpio

You should be in a position to make the most of the golden opportunities on offer. Those around you will be happy to support you during this exciting period, so go for it!

Look out for more
Silhouette Stars next month

SILHOUETTE
SPECIAL EDITION®

AVAILABLE FROM 22ND DECEMBER 2000

THE COWBOY AND THE NEW YEAR'S BABY
Sherryl Woods

That's My Baby! & And Baby Makes Three

Hardy Jones was as handsome as sin and sworn to be single. He knew nothing about delivering babies, but on New Year's Eve Trish Delacourt gave him a crash course!

A FAMILY HOMECOMING Laurie Paige

Montana

Kyle Mitchell had vowed to love, honour and cherish Danielle, yet it was more than two years since she—or their sweet child—had seen him. He'd come back to protect them, but would Danielle welcome him home?

A DOCTOR'S VOW Christine Rimmer

Prescription: Marriage

Hardworking paediatrician Veronica Powers was unnerved by her fascination with strong, sexy hospital administrator Ryan Malone—especially since his chaotic life involved three lively kids. But how could she resist them?

FALLING FOR AN OLDER MAN Trisha Alexander

Sheila Callahan had had an incurable crush on her brother's best friend Jack Kinsella for ages, and for just one moment the feeling seemed mutual. But all she was left with was heartache…and a little something more…

A COWBOY'S WOMAN Cathy Gillen Thacker

McCabe Men

The 'baby' of the McCabe brothers, Shane, had a reputation—in his work and with women. Rugged and wild, he swore he was never going to settle down; he'd even get married to prove it!

SOUL MATES Carol Finch

Her forbidden first love was back in town! No one had known that Katy and Nate were kindred spirits, only Katy and Nate remembered the passion they'd shared. Had Nate come back for her at last?

Fortune's Heirs

FREE

2 BOOKS
AND A SURPRISE GIFT!

We would like to take this opportunity to thank you for reading this Silhouette® book by offering you the chance to take TWO more specially selected titles from the Special Edition™ series absolutely FREE! We're also making this offer to introduce you to the benefits of the Reader Service™—

★ FREE home delivery ★ FREE gifts and competitions
★ FREE monthly Newsletter ★ Exclusive Reader Service discounts
★ Books available before they're in the shops

Accepting these FREE books and gift places you under no obligation to buy; you may cancel at any time, even after receiving your free shipment. Simply complete your details below and return the entire page to the address below. *You don't even need a stamp!*

YES! Please send me 2 free Special Edition books and a surprise gift. I understand that unless you hear from me, I will receive 4 superb new titles every month for just £2.70 each, postage and packing free. I am under no obligation to purchase any books and may cancel my subscription at any time. The free books and gift will be mine to keep in any case.

EOZEC

Ms/Mrs/Miss/Mr ....Initials...
BLOCK CAPITALS PLEASE

Surname..

Address...

....

....Postcode ....

Send this whole page to:
UK: FREEPOST CN81, Croydon, CR9 3WZ
EIRE: PO Box 4546, Kilcock, County Kildare (stamp required)

Offer valid in UK and Eire only and not available to current Reader Service subscribers to this series. We reserve the right to refuse an application and applicants must be aged 18 years or over. Only one application per household. Terms and prices subject to change without notice. Offer expires 30th June 2001. As a result of this application, you may receive further offers from Harlequin Mills & Boon Limited and other carefully selected companies. If you would prefer not to share in this opportunity please write to The Data Manager at the address above.

Silhouette® is a registered trademark used under license.
Special Edition™ is being used as a trademark.